BUZZ AROUND THE TRACK

They Said It

"I'm sick of playing by the rules. They haven't done me any good so far. Roberto Castillo is exactly what I need to change my image."
—Mallory Dalton

"There is nothing the press likes better than a good girl putting a bad boy on the straight and narrow."
—Roberto Castillo

"My wife and I have enough other things to worry about without having to concern ourselves with our new driver's love life."
—Dean Grosso

"Whether Roberto likes it or not, he's part of a team. He'd better start driving like it! Because with teammates like him, I don't need enemies."
—Kent Grosso

HELEN BRENNA

grew up the seventh of eight children in a small town in
central Minnesota. Although she never dreamed of writing
books, she's always been a voracious reader of romances.

After college, she started career life as an accountant, but
many years later the decision to stay home with her children
made all things possible, even writing the romances she still
loves to read.

Since Helen's first book was published in 2007, she's been
nominated for several awards, including *Romantic Times
BOOKreviews* Reviewer's Choice. Her books have won a Holt
Medallion and Romance Writers of America's prestigious
RITA® Award.

Helen continues to write away, living in Minnesota with her
husband, two children, two dogs and three surly (who can
blame them?) cats, and would love hearing from you. E-mail
her at helenbrenna@comcast.net or send mail to P.O. Box
24107, Minneapolis, MN 55424.

Visit her Web site at www.helenbrenna.com or chat with Helen
and other authors at RidingWithTheTopDown.blogspot.com.

||||||| NASCAR®

FROM THE OUTSIDE

Helen Brenna

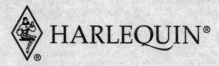

HARLEQUIN®

TORONTO • NEW YORK • LONDON
AMSTERDAM • PARIS • SYDNEY • HAMBURG
STOCKHOLM • ATHENS • TOKYO • MILAN • MADRID
PRAGUE • WARSAW • BUDAPEST • AUCKLAND

ISBN-13: 978-0-373-18522-1
ISBN-10:   0-373-18522-7

FROM THE OUTSIDE

Copyright © 2009 by Harlequin Books S.A.

Helen Brenna is acknowledged as the author of this work.

NASCAR® and the NASCAR Library Collection® are registered trademarks of the National Association for Stock Car Auto Racing, Inc.

www.eHarlequin.com

Printed in U.S.A.

Acknowledgments

I'm blessed to have people in my life who are wonderful resources and who so freely give of their time and talents. Without them, I'd have to write what I know, and how boring would that be?

Marsha Zinberg and Tina Colombo, without you two I would never have known I had this story in me. Thanks for bringing Roberto and Mallory into my life.

My heartfelt thanks to Tina Wexler for pushing me to make this book the best it could be.

A big holler out to my sister Mary Kuryla and her husband, Dennis, for keeping me in line on the racing details. And to my friend Mary Strand, who has on several occasions patiently helped me with Spanish translations. If there are errors, they can be placed at my stubborn doorstep.

Rosemary Heim, Christine Lashinski and Roxanne Richardson, I appreciate you guys never failing to tell me what's right, and wrong, with my books.

And finally, special thanks to Roberta Leighton for helping me in trying to understand the crazy life of an actress. May you stay forever young and restless!

NASCAR HIDDEN LEGACIES

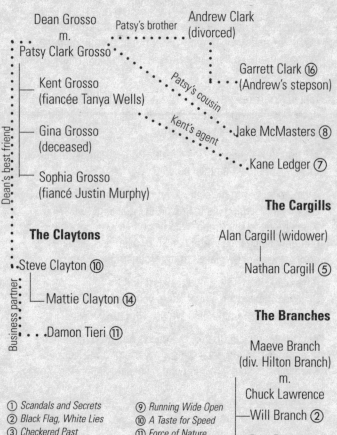

The Grossos

Dean Grosso
m.
Patsy Clark Grosso

— Kent Grosso
(fiancée Tanya Wells)

— Gina Grosso
(deceased)

— Sophia Grosso
(fiancé Justin Murphy)

Patsy's brother

The Clarks

Andrew Clark
(divorced)

Garrett Clark ⑯
(Andrew's stepson)

Patsy's cousin

Kent's agent

Jake McMasters ⑧

Kane Ledger ⑦

Dean's best friend

The Claytons

Steve Clayton ⑩

— Mattie Clayton ⑭

Damon Tieri ⑪

Business partner

The Cargills

Alan Cargill (widower)

Nathan Cargill ⑤

The Branches

Maeve Branch
(div. Hilton Branch)
m.
Chuck Lawrence

— Will Branch ②

— Bart Branch

— Penny Branch m.
Craig Lockhart

— Sawyer Branch

① *Scandals and Secrets*
② *Black Flag, White Lies*
③ *Checkered Past*
④ *From the Outside*
⑤ *Over the Wall*
⑥ *No Holds Barred*
⑦ *One Track Mind*
⑧ *Within Striking Distance*
⑨ *Running Wide Open*
⑩ *A Taste for Speed*
⑪ *Force of Nature*
⑫ *Banking on Hope*
⑬ *The Comeback*
⑭ *Into the Corner*
⑮ *Raising the Stakes*
⑯ *Crossing the Line*

THE FAMILIES AND THE CONNECTIONS

The Sanfords

Bobby Sanford
(deceased)
m.
Kath Sanford

— Adam Sanford ①

— Brent Sanford ⑫

— Trey Sanford ⑨

The Hunts

Dan Hunt
m.
Linda (Willard) Hunt
(deceased)

— Ethan Hunt ⑥

— Jared Hunt ⑮

— Hope Hunt ⑫

— Grace Hunt Winters ⑯
(widow of Todd Winters)

The Mathesons

Brady Matheson
(widower)
(fiancée Julie-Anne Blake)

— Chad Matheson ③

— Zack Matheson ⑬

— Trent Matheson
(fiancée Kelly Greenwood)

The Daltons

Buddy Dalton
m.
Shirley Dalton

— Mallory Dalton ④

— Tara Dalton ①

— Emma-Lea Dalton

CHAPTER ONE

SMACK!

The hand slapped across his cheek so fast Roberto Castillo had no time to react. *Wasn't the first time, wouldn't be the last.* He touched his stinging cheek and grinned. "What's the matter, Kacy? Can't stand the truth?"

"You bastard!" The sound of Kacy Haughton's voice was nearly lost amidst the typical Friday morning chaos of the Bellagio Hotel's main lobby. When she stomped her foot, his gaze was drawn, by no more than force of habit, to her cleavage.

Dios, ayúdele. Help me. Why in the world had he ever been attracted to these gorgeous, overindulged, high-maintenance women?

"We are so finished!" she spat at him between a set of glossy pink lips.

Funny. As far as Roberto was concerned, there was nothing between them to finish. No matter what she or the press seemed to think, he and Kacy had never been dating. Several months back, she'd latched on to him like grime on a *gaucho,* showing up at clubs and casinos he occasionally frequented, finagling infield passes to his races and not so quietly infiltrating his life.

He'd finally had enough and told her to back off, but she'd probably been too drunk to remember that conversation, the one after that and the one after that. The woman partied so much that he'd been surprised to come down from his Tower Suite a few moments ago and find her not only awake at nine in the morning, but completely accessorized. She'd been waiting for him as he headed toward his meeting with his agent.

"Go ahead and smirk all you want," she said, glaring at him.

Clearly fighting to maintain an upper hand, she tossed back her long, natural blond hair. "By the time I'm done, the press will be slicing and dicing you."

She flicked her fingers in the air, summoning someone to their corner of the lobby. A man with a digital camera in his hand came running across the polished marble floor. "Did you get it?" she asked.

"Yup." The young man nodded. "Still frames and video."

"Perfect." She dismissed the photographer with another flip of her wrist.

"You set me up," Roberto said, not the least bit surprised.

"God, I'm going to miss that sexy Argentinean accent," she said, slipping on a pair of rhinestone-studded sunglasses. "But I never asked for much, Roberto. Just a little attention." She strode toward the outside exit. "See you in tomorrow's paper."

Perfecto. Exactly what he did not need. More fodder for the late-night-talk-show hosts.

He tugged on the neck of his black T-shirt, loosening the fit, and glanced around the opulent setting of elegant water fountains, stained-glass skylight and monstrous exotic plant displays, wondering how many people had noticed Kacy's tantrum. No one's feathers looked particularly ruffled. Apparently, the sight of the spoiled-rotten offspring of a Silicon Valley magnate slapping open-wheel's biggest playboy didn't warrant much attention.

Vegas. Gotta love this place.

But then, he had to quit thinking of himself as an open-wheel driver. He was NASCAR now, all the way. And playboy? No matter how he tried deluding himself to the contrary, the over-thirty Roberto Castillo couldn't hold a candle to the escapades of the younger men. Not even a flicker of a flame. Open-wheel racing wasn't the only thing for which he'd gotten too old.

The sound of clapping echoed off the walls and ceiling of the cavernous lobby. He spun around to find his agent, Patricia Brink, a tall, spindly thin woman in her midfifties—he could never get an exact age out of her—slapping her hands together in a slow, methodical beat. "That was quite a show." Her thin smile barely caused a wrinkle. "What're you doing for an encore?"

"Oh, I don't know." He walked toward her. "Got any tricks up your sleeves? I'm open to suggestions."

Patricia crossed her arms. "No matter how flippant you'd like to be about this situation, that woman's hand connecting with your face is not going to look pretty in tomorrow's papers." She wore a loose-fitting, extravagantly embroidered silver tunic and pale gray pants, designed to portray, to anyone who didn't know her, a carefree, hippie look. "It might be considered juicy enough to make it in tonight's entertainment news."

"Have pity on me. I am a poor moth and extreme women my ever-loving flame."

"Yeah, right." She rolled her eyes. "You might be able to fool the rest of the world, but I've known you too long, Roberto. These days, three-quarters of what the media says about you isn't even close to the truth and you don't do a damned thing about it."

Because he liked it that way. People thought they knew who he was, but these days, the lies provided the only kind of privacy Roberto could count on anymore.

"This time, though, I'm afraid they might be right." Patricia raised her eyebrows. "I saw the way you grinned at Kacy before she wound up and planted one on your face."

Old habits died hard. But no woman liked to be told she was a lush. Roberto's father would've been ashamed of him for speaking to a woman—any woman—in that fashion, and the thought of *Papá* sent a shot of sobering guilt through him.

"*Tienes razón,*" he agreed. "You are right. I did deserve it. So now what?"

"File a restraining order against our dear Miss Haughton. Trash her in the press. And get her, once and for all, out of the picture."

Beat a dog when it was down? He glanced away. Not his style. "No."

"Why not?" Clearly frustrated, she shook her head, and thick chunks of her shoulder-length gray hair fell forward with the motion. "The Grossos are going to be extremely upset when they see those pictures. They may have grounds to cancel your contract."

Dean and Patsy were nice, solid people and he couldn't fault them for wanting the reputation of their company, Cargill-Grosso Racing, to reflect their own straightforward, family-oriented values. The only reason they'd signed Roberto as their newest driver was because Patricia had busted her butt convincing them that he would thoroughly clean up his act. Unfortunately, no matter how low-key Roberto had kept his personal life these past few months, a decade or more of player antics in international open-wheel racing still clung to him like black on a panther.

That was no reason to lash out at a sad and pathetic young woman. "I won't trash her," he said.

"I had a feeling you'd say that. Good thing I've already set another plan in motion." Patricia sighed and made a show of studying him from head to toe. "Haven't you heard the grunge look is out?"

He ignored the reference to his faded shirt and jeans. These days, when he wasn't at the track, comfort was all he cared about. "Another plan?"

"Come on, pretty boy." She dragged him toward the exit. "After today, with any degree of luck, Miss Haughton's little stunt will cause barely a ripple in the pond."

"What am I doing today?"

"I'll explain on the way."

He climbed into a waiting limo behind his agent and held his breath as their driver pulled out onto The Strip. This couldn't be good, especially since she wouldn't tell him anything over the phone last night about her meeting with the Grossos to discuss ideas for marketing him to the American public.

"Where are we going?" he asked.

"Caesars Palace." She studied him as if she was deciding on her approach. Finally, she said, "Look. I know you're only a few races into the season, but Dean and Patsy are more than a little worried. It's one thing to drop from a starting position of fifth at

Daytona down to twenty-third at the finish, but bumping Kent Grosso, your own teammate, in California looked bad."

"It happens."

"Tell that to Kent. He's still pissed off."

"They can't expect miracles."

"I know." She held out her hand. "Transitioning into stock car racing is difficult."

"Exactly."

In open-wheel, winning was more about technology and a driver's hand to eye coordination than anything else. Hell, the damned steering wheels were programmed with engine mapping, tracking controls and adaptive suspension, all at the tip of a driver's fingertips. And no one had been faster at it than Roberto. For years, he'd dominated in the highest levels of open-wheel racing, but then he'd hit thirty and suddenly winning wasn't the only thing that mattered. Better to get out at the top of his game than become complacent.

"You know I am a good driver, Patricia. I need some time to adjust."

"Time alone isn't going to cut it, and you know it. NASCAR's very different from the kind of driving you were used to."

He was only now understanding how different, and no small part of him was worried. His palms suddenly sweating, he turned toward the window, only marginally aware of the lane on top of lane of cars zipping this way and that, of the casinos glistening under the hot, March Nevada sunshine.

"Like it or not, this has to be said," Patricia continued. "If you don't figure out how to be a team player fast, you're not going to make it in stock car racing."

Although he'd been hungry for a new challenge and more competition, he hadn't counted on how important teamwork was to a NASCAR driver's performance. He fixed his gaze on the smooth trunks of tall palms towering above the grassy median. "Let me worry about my driving."

"All right," she agreed. "As long as you let me worry about your image."

She had him. In the palm of her hand. She was good. "Okay. You have me." He turned toward her. "What is your plan?"

"Something drastic." She smiled. "Considering we didn't count on how much the media loves their bad boys, I think I've hit on a quick fix."

"There is no such thing. And you know it."

"This one's simple. A little unorthodox, but you might actually have some fun this time."

"Quit flitting around the deal. What is it?"

"Five cameo appearances in an American daytime drama. It's new, but very popular."

Dios. A soap opera. Over the past decade-plus, he'd made appearances and enough commercial spots in Europe, Asia and in his home country of Argentina to be wary of stupid storylines and worse dialogue.

"If you don't like it," she said, smiling, "we could always spotlight your charity work. The free medical clinic. The food shelves. The homeless and battered women's shelters. The foundation providing more college scholarsh—"

"No." He hated it when celebrities put themselves out there as some kind of saviors. *"En absoluto."* He'd been given a lot. He had a lot to give back. That's all there was to it.

"All right, then. Soap opera it is." She handed him a stack of papers from her briefcase along with a pen. "It's all ready to sign."

After reading everything, he signed where indicated and handed the contracts back.

"Come on, lighten up," she said. "It's for the show *Racing Hearts.* You'll be playing yourself, so you'll have fun. I promise."

"Now? This morning?"

"Yep." She handed him what looked like a script. "They wanted you for tomorrow, but your schedule is full until Sunday's race. You're free this morning, but qualifying this afternoon?"

"Sí."

He'd only had a few minutes to read through some of his lines before their limo circled a water fountain surrounded by marble statues in front of Caesars Palace and parked at the entrance.

Handlers met them at the doors and swiftly escorted them to a section of the casino floor that had been cordoned off from the public. Several bigwig production people, producers and directors made their way to where Patricia and he were standing and introduced themselves. They thanked him profusely, explained a bit of what would be happening and went on with their business.

A woman, presumably the show's costume person, came to within a few feet of them and, obviously disgusted, put her hands out to her sides. "What's with the faded jeans and T-shirt? You were supposed to wear a black suit coat and white dress shirt."

"Must have missed that memo."

She disappeared for a few minutes and came back carrying the aforementioned garments. "These oughta fit."

When he raised his eyebrows at her, Patricia said, "Roberto. Please."

"Fine." Right there, he drew his T-shirt over his head, stuffed his arms into the starched sleeves of the dress shirt, and shrugged on the suit coat, hating the feel of this stiff fabric.

The wardrobe lady reached toward him. "May I?"

"May you what?"

"Fix your shirt?"

"Whatever."

She closed him up, leaving a couple buttons undone on top, and stepped back. "Tuck."

"Excuse me?"

"Tuck it in. Unless you'd like me to do it for you."

Meat, that's all he was. He shoved the shirttails into his jeans. "How's that?"

"Close." She undid another button and then actually fluffed his chest hair.

He grinned. "I hear this hotel has private rooms."

"Maybe later." Arching her eyebrows, she spun around. "I'll send makeup over."

"Behave." Patricia pinched him.

"Aí." He grabbed his arm. "Why should I?"

"Because women always think you're serious."

"Maybe I am. She was kinda cute."

As Patricia rolled her eyes, another woman, the makeup lady, escorted him to a director's chair in front of a mirror. She covered the collar of his dress shirt with a protective towel and then slathered on a layer of thick makeup. When she reached for his head, he pulled back.

"I need to fix your hair," she explained.

"My hair's fine." Pancake batter on his face he could handle. A few quick swipes with a hot washcloth and it was gone, but he hated anyone touching his head. Most people thought he was vain for keeping his hair long enough to just pull it into a ponytail. The reality was, he couldn't tolerate people touching his head.

"Some spray?" She held out a can.

"Over my dead body."

"Suit yourself." With a shrug of her shoulders and a last-minute suggestion to pay attention to the prompters, she walked off.

He finished reading his script and rejoined Patricia, more than a little disgusted with how they'd planned on portraying him in the show. "This stint is not going to help my image."

"Yes, it will."

"They have me coming on to one of their female leads. In a casino. Doesn't sound very redeeming to me."

"They've assured me that you eventually end up helping that character break off her engagement to a cheating jerk," Patricia explained.

"So I'm to be a savior?" That would be the day. Roberto shook his head. All he wanted to do was race. *Give me my No. 507 car. Please.*

"And here's the best part," she said, smiling. "You'll be playing opposite Mallory Dalton."

He'd heard of her and had seen her on the trailer in a bit part for an upcoming movie. "America's Sweetheart," he said. *Americano querida.* Now this was all making sense. "Smart move."

"If this works the way I think it will, you'll be able to stop worrying about your image and start focusing on your driving."

Several women stepped onto the set and the makeup person put finishing touches on their hair and faces. After studying the group, Roberto picked out Mallory. She was pretty, but not as gorgeous as he'd expected. With a genuine smile, black hair that fell in soft curls to the middle of her back and dark eyes that twinkled with every flash of light, she looked every bit the girl next door. Her style of clothing—a loose-fitting white blouse and unremarkable black pants—sealed the deal. She was young, too. Her sweet baby face made him wonder if she was legal drinking age.

"Are you sure this is going to work?" he whispered to Patricia. "She looks more innocent than Vegas nights are long."

"I know. Isn't it great?" Patricia's face brightened. "If she can't scrub that playboy grime right off your thick, tarnished hide, then no one can. That's why part two of my plan is so brilliant."

"Part two?" *Oh, hell.*

"Her agent and I worked out a deal. You and Mallory Dalton have your first date tonight."

"What?" Roberto rounded on her. "I make my own arrangements with women, thank you very much."

"No, you don't. You'd just like everyone to think you do."

She had him on that count. For more than a year, he'd sworn off women and booze and everything in between. Livin' *la vida tranquila,* and he kind of liked it. "That woman is clearly not my type."

"She's beautiful."

"Angelic is more like it, and she doesn't do a thing for me."

"You could do with some innocence in your love life."

"Innocence is another way of saying boring."

"That's only because you have the attention span of a gnat where women are concerned. You're going!"

"No, I'm not."

"The Grossos signed off on this."

"They wouldn't have."

"How do you know?"

"Because cameo appearances on soap operas are one thing. Arranging a romance goes too far. That, Patricia *estimada,* is something only you would cook up."

"Okay, so they didn't know about the dating part, but you are making too much of this. All I'm asking is for you to hang out with an actress. What can be so hard about that? She's a woman. How innocent can she be?"

He wasn't going to touch that one.

"Her first movie's coming out shortly and the critics are raving about her small but pivotal role. She has a lot of visibility right now, and, most important, America loves her. All you need to do is be seen together. Get photographed together. Rub off on each other."

"I am not rubbing anything on that young woman. I'd probably scare her half to death."

"Any guesses how the Grossos will react when Kacy Haughton's pictures hit the gossip columns tomorrow?"

Roberto clenched his teeth and accepted the fact that he was cornered. It was his own damned fault. Again. "*Bueno.* Fine. One date. That is it."

"Oh, no, Roberto, dear. I've got your entire weekend planned out."

CHAPTER TWO

OH. MY. GOD.

Mallory Dalton concentrated on making herself breathe. Roberto Castillo, *the* Roberto Castillo, stood no more than thirty feet away. Her parents, diehard NASCAR fans, weren't going to believe this. Her youngest sister, Emma-Lee, was going to scream over the phone when she found out Mallory would be on the same set with the man, right next to him, talking with him, no less than *five* times. Her middle sister, Tara, had declared on several occasions that while she wouldn't trade her new fiancé, Adam Sanford, for any man in the world, Roberto had to be the sexiest driver in NASCAR history. Mallory, on the other hand, couldn't stand the man.

Well, that wasn't entirely true. He was, arguably, one of the world's best drivers, having won more open-wheel championships in his career than anyone in the history of the sport, so it was difficult to not respect his performance as a driver. Since he'd jumped to this side of the pond, she'd watched his races and cheered him on.

But as a person? So he was attractive. And for once he was wearing a suit. Looked awfully good in it, too. There wasn't much else to like. Arrogant, overconfident and a playboy to the nth degree, the man was full of himself.

"He's hot!" one of Mallory's female costars whispered. "Where has that man been all my life?"

Give it time, Mallory wanted to say. *Eventually, he's bound to make it around to you.*

The makeup artist came toward them, brush and powder in

hand. "If you ladies plan on eating anything, do it now before I touch you up." She pointed to the small table filled with juices, coffees and rolls.

"In my dreams," one of the women said, looking longingly at a plump, chocolate-covered doughnut.

"I'd rather dream about Latino men," another actress commented as powder was brushed onto her nose. "I could listen to that accent all day long."

Oh, for God's sake. Mallory bit her tongue. Roberto Castillo barely looked Latino. Sure, he had dark hair, eyes and skin, but with a narrow nose and face, his mother's Italian roots had clearly come through. And his longish, curly hair made him look more European than anything. Apparently, Argentina had the highest concentration of European immigrants among South American countries. She must have read that somewhere, possibly in a biography, or maybe a travel guide. Though her passport had yet to be stamped, she was ever hopeful an opportunity would present itself.

"Your turn." The brush lady moved around to the next woman.

"Mallory, you're so lucky," the first actress commented. "You'll probably get to kiss him in one of your upcoming scenes."

She thought of all the places that man's mouth had likely been and grimaced. Heavy into a conversation with an older woman with thick gray hair, presumably his agent, Roberto glanced over and caught her staring at his lips. An involuntary sound escaped her throat, and she quickly looked away.

"You okay?" someone asked.

"Fine," she squeaked. Love them or hate them, some people were simply larger than life. For lack of anything better to do, she grabbed a plain doughnut, shoved half of it in her mouth and washed it down with a glug of coffee.

Her costars stared at her. "After that, I'd have to starve myself for the rest of the day," one of them said.

Hollywood skinny be damned. To spite them all, Mallory poured some half-and-half into her coffee. And she didn't even like cream.

"Roberto, we're ready for you," the director yelled. "Come on over."

"Your turn, Mallory." The makeup artist touched Mallory's chin, turning her face, and made a sigh of disgust. "If I've told you once, dear, I've told you a thousand times, ditch the neutral lip balm. Lack of color makes you look washed-out on the screen." She swiped a crimson-colored cream over Mallory's lips and handed her the tube. "Red or at least pink from now on, okay?"

"But it makes my lips look so big." She hated standing out.

"That's exactly the point." The woman walked away, throwing one final comment over her shoulder. "Do you realize how much some women *pay* for that look?"

Why anyone would want to poof herself up with collagen was beyond Mallory. She spun back around to find Roberto coming straight toward their group from the other side of the set.

Okay. Showtime.

"Hello, ladies," he said with only a hint of an accent. Occasionally, when he was interviewed on TV and he was in a hurry or very excited, his enunciation was as thick and rich as chocolate syrup. She had the distinct impression he purposefully toned it down most of the time.

"Hi," the other women said, practically in unison.

Mallory didn't bother opening her mouth. Better he didn't notice her at all. She was fine, comfortable even, hanging out in the proverbial woodwork.

"I am Roberto Castillo." He glanced from one actress to the next, his gaze appreciative, although the look he gave her was curiously indecipherable. "And consider myself very fortunate to be working with such a lovely cast."

Gag me.

Her coworkers turned into gushing puddles of feminine goo.

"I've never met a race car driver before."

"What's it like?"

"Don't you get scared?"

On and on they went. It was all Mallory could do not to choke on all the syrupy sweetness. Thank heavens the director intervened to clarify for Roberto how the production process worked for daytime dramas. Three cameras would be arranged around the set and any one of them might be filming at any given moment. While the assistant director would be handling the action on set, the director and producers would be in a booth watching several monitors and deciding when and from what angle each of the cameras would be taping. A prompter would be within Roberto's line of sight in case he forgot what to say.

"Okay, let's go, people," the director said. He came to stand next to Mallory. "Here's the deal." He put his hand on her shoulder. "You're on a girls' weekend away. Playing up the slots with your buds. Roberto, you see Mallory. And you're attracted. Her character's engaged to be married to a boy back home. But he's a jerk. Everyone hates him. The point of your cameos on our show is for you to become the catalyst she needs to break off a bad engagement.

"Today, all you have to do, Roberto, is ask her out to dinner. Then we move to the restaurant scene. Okay?" He glanced at each of them in turn. "Everyone ready?"

Mallory went to her designated chair at her designated slot machine and closed her eyes for a moment, letting herself sink into character. Initially, something inside her resisted. She was so done with this sickeningly sweet persona. *Not much longer, Mal, and you'll be moving on.*

The director went back to his booth and the assistant director went to work. "All right, people," he said. "Settle."

That was the order for the cast to take their predetermined positions and get ready. Mallory's stomach did a somersault, the way it always did before taping began, and then she felt herself being wrapped in layers of surreal calm.

"Quiet on the set." Activity in the rest of the casino caused a hum of background noise. "Rolling. Five, four, three, two, one, and…" He signaled with the fingers of his hand for the scene to start taping.

Mallory slid a bill into the slot machine, pretending to be happy about it. Her costars, standing next to her, were talking and laughing, but she was supposed to be oblivious, mesmerized by the slot machine.

As if. She'd never been in a casino before this week and couldn't imagine why anyone might find this particular activity entertaining. Mindless and boring. As all get-out. She pressed a few more buttons. Blackjack, Texas Hold 'Em and craps—now those were games that sounded like fun.

She sensed rather than saw Roberto leaning against her slot machine. "*Buenos días,* ladies," he said.

Mallory kept her focus on the dials spinning in front of her.

"You are working that machine over pretty hard, little lady," he said. "Any luck?"

The other women elbowed her, whispering, "It's Roberto Castillo. You know, the *NASCAR* driver."

"Who?" Mallory glanced up and tried to capture the feeling she'd had when he'd first spoken to her group only moments before. She didn't have to try very hard. One look directly into his eyes and the breath whooshed out of her lungs. "Oh, my! Hello."

"*Buenos días,*" he said, his gaze focused only on her.

At that moment she understood why women went gaga over him. When he focused directly on her, she felt like the only person in the world. Special. Maybe even beautiful.

Her first instinct was to slough it off, but she couldn't let herself. This is what her character was supposed to feel. She absorbed it, embraced it. Her *Racing Hearts* persona was eventually going to cancel a wedding over this man. A catalyst, the director had called him. And he was. She only wished her character could stand on her own two feet without a handsome, articulate and sexy man by her side.

They finished the first scene and Mallory was delighted when Roberto ad-libbed his own dialogue over some of the worst pickup lines she'd ever read in her life. In between the next scene and the next, he joked with the cast and crew, setting everyone at ease. About two hours later, they were finished.

"Okay. That's a wrap on Mr. Castillo's scenes," the director said from his booth. "Everyone take ten. Roberto, thank you very much. We won't need you back on set for a few weeks. Mallory, wonderful job. As always, you were the quintessential girl next door."

"Yeah, about that." Mallory barely kept herself from rolling her eyes at the director. "Have you given any thought to letting my character take a few steps out on the wild side?"

"We're thinking about it, Mal. Give it time."

That's all she could ask.

Roberto nodded to Mallory, his gaze once more unreadable. "I look forward to working with you again, Miss Dalton." He rejoined the older woman waiting for him at the edge of the set.

That's when Mallory noticed her agent, Theo Stein, speed walking toward Roberto. Tall and slim with thick-framed glasses and hair so gray it was almost white, Theo looked more like a fashion designer than anything. He motioned with his index finger for her to join their group.

Shaking off the layers of her *Racing Hearts* character, she headed toward them. "Theo?" Strange, he hadn't called to let her know he'd be in town. "What are you doing here?"

"Negotiating a deal for you."

"What deal?" Mallory glanced from Roberto to his agent and back to Theo. All of them seemed privy to some secret information.

"A date with Roberto Castillo," Theo said.

What!

"You didn't already discuss this with her?" Roberto's agent glared impatiently at Theo.

"Why should I? She knows I would only recommend opportunities that are in her best interest."

She owed everything to Theo. He'd been her agent from the get-go, single-handedly turning small-town Mary-Jean Dalton into Mallory, a relatively successful TV actress. She'd spent a few years floundering from one job to the next after graduating from high school and was waitressing in a Mooresville restaurant when he'd discovered her and subsequently convinced a TV director to cast her as the middle daughter on a wholesome family drama. She'd played fresh-faced Amy Mitchell, a character eight years her junior, for many years before the cast split and she'd moved on to other naive characters in other wholesome TV gigs. She'd started on *Racing Hearts* a little more than a year ago.

Since the beginning, Theo had meticulously selected modeling gigs, product endorsements and acting roles in order to cultivate Mallory's image. *Branding,* Theo always said, made for solid, steady work. Mallory had another name for it—typecasting. If she didn't do something about it soon, she'd be playing green young women until her baby-faced looks caught up with her age and her acting career would be as good as over.

Theo glanced at his watch. "Let's get this deal done. I've got lunch with a prospect."

With a sigh, the older woman turned to Mallory. "I'm Patricia Brink, dear, Roberto's agent." Absently, Mallory shook the woman's hand. "We have a proposition we think you'll be interested in." She went on to describe what sounded no more than a publicity stunt flawed in its fundamental premise that Roberto, a man considered one of the most eligible bachelors in the world, might possibly be interested in her.

"You're suggesting that *Roberto* wants to be seen with *me?*" Mallory glanced at Roberto and realized he didn't. Not in the slightest. She swallowed, suddenly feeling smaller than before.

"Well, to be honest, it was my idea," Patricia said. "Not Roberto's."

That made sense. In truth, he wasn't her type any more than she presumed she was his. But there was another problem with their plan. "Why should anyone give a hoot what I do?"

"You kidding?" Patricia put out her hands and the large bangles at her wrist clattered. "You're America's Sweetheart."

Sweetheart. Right. Mallory barely kept herself from snorting out loud. But if she wasn't an amalgamation of all the virtuous characters she'd played through the years, then who was she? Exactly?

That was the question she'd been burning to answer most of her life, and that's what had drawn her to acting. It should have given her the opportunity to try on different hats and faces, be different people. Someday, maybe, she'd get back to the business of finally figuring out who she was. Exactly.

"What about Kacy Haughton?" Mallory asked. "I thought—"

"No," Roberto said with a quick shake of his head. "We were never dating."

"But the news—"

"Is wrong," he said. "You can't always believe what you read or see on TV."

"Okay, so Kacy's history," she said. "I still don't get it."

"There's nothing to get, Mallory. You can use this exposure now. Before you audition for that romantic comedy," Theo said, his eyes darting back and forth as if he were making constant calculations in his head. "Roberto scratches your back. You scratch his." The way he said it made the potential deal sound more tawdry than before.

Maybe she wouldn't need her back scratched if she broke out of this mold Theo kept pouring her into. She didn't want to work on another light comedy. *Did you even read that script my friend gave me?* That was the movie she wanted to work on next, the part of the prodigal sister in an edgy and dark independent movie called *Three Sisters* that would soon be taking auditions. Playing a recovering drug addict would finally give her the opportunity to prove she could really act. Wouldn't that be something?

"Maybe we should let these two talk." As if she could sense Mallory's growing hostility toward her own agent, Patricia dragged Theo several feet away.

Suddenly, she found herself alone with a man who'd been consistently voted among the top ten sexiest men alive. Instead of coming on to her like he did to every other woman who could walk, talk or breathe, he was studying her like a bug he'd as soon squash as anything.

The seconds ticked by without either of them saying anything. Finally, Mallory gathered her nerve. "I'm not interested." She couldn't believe it, but she actually turned her back on him. *The* Roberto Castillo.

What had gotten into her?

"Hey, wait a minute," Roberto whispered close behind her. "Mallory."

Oh...my...God. His accent, his breathy *H*'s, the way his words flowed into one another like silk against suede, the way he said her name, softly rolling the *R,* had her almost pooling onto the floor in what would no doubt be a mound of loose joints.

"Forget our agents," he said. "You and I...should talk."

She turned back around. "I'm listening."

Casually, he leaned against the wall. "You would like to break into movies, correct?"

She nodded. "I just finished my first one. A small role, but I'm hoping for a larger, supporting part next time around."

He nodded. "It takes time to go in new directions. But there are some things you can do to speed along the process. A lot will depend on your reception at the box office, correct?"

"Probably."

"When will the movie be released?"

"Next month."

"You see? Perfect timing. You and I spend time together. We get your name in the press before the premiere. Generate a buzz. You do great at the box office. And you land a supporting role in your next film. Like that." He took her hand between both of his and warmed her cold fingers.

Another time and place, the motion might've been comforting. But here, now, it seemed practiced, designed to tease and control. Unable to think straight while he was touching her, let alone looking at her as if she were a hot new sports car and he couldn't wait to shift her gears, she stuffed her hands into the pockets of her dress pants.

"I'm not sure the publicity would be good for my reputation," she said. "Besides, what's in it for you?"

"I have been in the public eye a very long while." His smile was a little lopsided. "There is nothing the press likes better than a good girl putting a bad boy on the straight and narrow. That story is as old as time."

Her thoughts bounced back and forth, the pros and cons. One

minute, she could see the logic in his proposal, and then it seemed preposterous. "I'm sorry, but you and me... I...don't do bad boys."

"Are you sure?" He grinned his trademark smile, complete with a dimple in his left cheek.

She swallowed. "I'm very flattered—"

"One date. We'll go from there. There's no harm in giving this a shot, is there?" He gazed at her as if she were an ice-cream cone. She was dripping and he was going to lick her up.

Oh, Lord. She put out her hand, palm toward him as if to fend him off. "You and I both know you could sleep with any woman on this set. Why me?"

"No one said anything about sleeping together," he whispered. "Although I certainly won't complain if you are offering."

Good grief. "I'm not." Was there anyone out there more arrogant than this man?

He laughed then, a sound as smooth and rich as a mocha latte. "I am that distasteful to you?"

"That's not what I meant."

"It's all right. I appreciate your honesty. But we are only suggesting you and I do some things together this weekend. Completely legitimate things. Go out to dinner. Catch a show. You come to my race on Sunday. If the publicity seems to be working for both of us, we can talk about extending the deal a few weeks.

"More dinners. More races. I will attend your functions. Like your premiere. Or whatever it is you like to do. The point is to be seen together. We should both get mileage from that kind of publicity."

"Pretending."

"Basically."

"It sounds awfully manipulative. Fake. I'm not sure I'd be very good—"

"You are an actress. All you have to do is pretend we are on camera."

The way he said *actress* made it sound like an insult. "What if it doesn't work?"

"I am not asking you to spend the rest of your life with me. This is about the two of us capitalizing on each other's popularity, on our public images. For a short while. Think of it as a…business arrangement without an ounce of commitment. If it works, great. If it does not, *así es*. No harm in trying."

"What are you worried about, Mallory?" Theo said, coming back to them. "Relax. Have fun. Dinner and a show. What could be more harmless?" He shrugged. "You need to do this."

What she *needed* was a backbone.

She glanced back and forth between Theo and Roberto. Theo made no bones about pressuring her. Roberto looked as if he couldn't care less whether or not she went along with the plan. In fact, she almost sensed he'd be somehow relieved if she didn't. Patricia had kept a slight distance, but Mallory could feel her studying, appraising, calculating.

Mallory wanted a lead role in a movie, and yet, she didn't trust any one of these three people standing in front of her to help her achieve her goals any further than she could throw them. The truth was that for most of her life, she'd been letting other people make decisions for her. First, her parents, her teachers, close friends, even her younger sisters. And then Theo. A personal direction had never seemed clear. This was more of the same.

Or was it?

Theo could be wrong. This thing could backfire on all of them. They were all making one critical mistake. They assumed she liked being America's Sweetheart.

Mentally stepping back and away, Mallory imagined how this deal might play out with a little tweaking. If she played this right, Roberto Castillo could very well help her prove to the world that she wasn't sweet little Amy Mitchell any longer.

"Bottom line?" Theo said, impatient. "This is good for your career."

Bottom line? She had nothing to lose and everything to gain. "All right," she said. "It's a deal."

"Good." Theo handed one document to her and another to

Roberto. "Here's your agenda. Stick to it. Roberto will pick you up tonight at seven."

Mallory smiled inside. "See you then."

Roberto didn't know it yet, but he was the key to breaking the sweetheart stranglehold America had on her throat.

CHAPTER THREE

ROBERTO STOOD in the lobby of Mallory's hotel, waiting for her to come down for their big *date,* thinking of any number of things he'd rather be doing than going to dinner and a show with Miss Goody Two-shoes. Heading back to his own hotel room to read and catch a solid night's sleep before practice tomorrow held more appeal than a night on the town.

Only thirty years old, and already he felt bored to tears with this world. There had to be something he could do to make this obligatory night more interesting. Car show? He doubted she'd be interested. Club dancing? The only things Mallory Dalton probably ever shook were salt and pepper containers. Casinos? America's Sweetheart? Right.

Dinner and a show it was.

Besides, Theo Stein had meticulously planned the evening out for them with a mind toward the quiet and staid, and, for a place like Vegas, that was quite an achievement. He'd also contacted a photographer or two, delighted with the potential for tonight's photo ops.

No shenanigans, Patricia had said, adding her two cents. She'd ordered Roberto to be on his best behavior. Or else. And to make sure he looked good while he was being good, she'd had a black suit and pale pink dress shirt delivered to his suite with a note attached that read, *Yes, I'll be adding these to your next bill, but try to wear them with a pleasant smile.*

The clothes might fit like a dream and be made of the softest silk, but they weren't him. Not even close. The least Patricia could've done was found him a shirt with bold stripes or a flashy print to ease the sting of wearing a suit.

Roberto's cell phone rang, and he glanced at the display. His mother. *Perfecto*. This night couldn't get any better. In the past few days, she'd left him no fewer than ten messages, and he'd yet to return any of them. He glanced at his watch. He had a few minutes. Might as well get this over and done with.

Hoping to be as inconspicuous as possible, he ducked beneath the shade of a potted palm. *"Hola, Madre."*

"You are not winning your races," she said, ever the doting mother.

"Really? Thanks for the play-by-play."

"NASCAR," she muttered. "You were the driver to beat in open-wheel racing. Why change?"

He had to be honest with her. With himself. "I'll be thirty-one soon, *Madre*. The international circuits are for young men."

"You are not old. Roberto Castillo Franco is the best driver alive."

There she went again, tacking her last name onto his. In many Latin countries, it was customary for a child's formal name to include his mother's, but Camila had only offered him her last name after he'd won his first open-wheel race. At the time, Roberto been twenty-three and on his way to passing out from all the champagne, so he'd probably been appropriately teary-eyed and grateful, but, to this day, Castillo was Roberto's legal name and the only one he ever intended to use.

"And I would like to stay alive," he said. "Or would you rather I get killed making a stupid mistake?" Then he remembered who he was speaking to, a mother who never wanted to be a mother in the first place. "Wait a minute. Don't answer that."

"Roberto. How can you say that?"

"Look. The bottom line is that there's more to racing than winning. It's as simple as that. I needed more competition."

"And you get that with restrictor plates?" she asked.

"Sí. They help create more serious competition," he argued. "Once I pull ahead in open-wheel, at best, one or two cars can

pass me. In NASCAR, it's not uncommon for ten different cars to lead any given race. And toward the end of the regular season, the points are wiped out and the playing field is leveled for the top twelve drivers. *That* is the kind of competition I'm talking about."

He didn't know why he bothered explaining things to her.

It was his father's fault, really. Luis Castillo had never said one bad thing about Camila Franco during Roberto's childhood. All he'd ever talked about was how Camila had taken his breath away the first time he'd seen her in the stables at the seaside resort where he'd worked at the time. His father had always said it'd been love at first sight for both of them. To this day, Roberto had never been able to figure out why his father had lied to him, claiming that Camila had died in childbirth. What a pathetic romantic, his father.

"You know, you should respect me more," his mother went on. "And do what I say. If it was not for me, you would not be where you are today."

Well, that was probably very true, but not in the way she meant. He was where he was today in *spite* of her.

"*Madre,* I am not going back to open-wheel. Ever. I'll continue to send you tickets to all my NASCAR races. It's up to you whether or not you come."

"Do you want me to come?"

What a loaded question. He could never forget his immense satisfaction the first time his mother had come to one of his races. Knowing she was there had spurred him on. He'd made his first track-record speed that day and won. For her. But he could also never wipe out her look of disdain the first time his own error had cost him a race.

He thought he'd dealt with this issue years ago. Instead, it crept up on him, this intense need for her love and approval, and often blindsided him at the strangest and most unexpected moments. Quite clearly, he knew it for what it was. A boy's need for a mother's love. Was there any stronger love in the world? He thought he'd accepted it was something he'd never experience in this lifetime. Apparently not.

Push, pull. Love, hate. Black, white. Conflicted and contradictory, that was the only way to describe his relationship with his mother. The really odd thing was that Roberto had never felt compelled to send race tickets to his father, a man he loved without question.

"Well?" his mother said. "Do you want me to come to the race or not?"

"Come or don't come," he said. *"No me importa."*

But they both knew he did care.

He'd no sooner disconnected the call than Mallory came away from the elevators and headed toward the exit. She didn't immediately see him, so he had a moment to watch her.

She looked nervous and insecure. There was something else there, too, something he couldn't put a finger on. She'd surprised him back at the *Racing Hearts* set by initially turning down the offer for some free publicity. He'd surprised himself by liking that about her, not to mention the relish with which she devoured doughnuts and creamed coffee.

Patricia, on the other hand, had a different take. "Watch yourself with her," she'd said after their meeting that morning. "I don't trust that woman."

"Worried about me, Patricia? How sweet."

"Go ahead and laugh. She's hard to read."

She was at that. "She's an actress," Roberto had countered. If the short scenes he'd done with her were any indication, a darned good one at that.

He was struck, again, by the possibilities Mallory presented. So much potential wrapped in the wrong packaging. This afternoon, she'd worn plain, baggy clothing. Tonight, although she was still beautiful and her dress clung more closely to her curves, the skirt was too long, reaching below her knees, and the fabric was baby-blue, an altogether too pale a hue for Mallory's coloring, making her look a bit sallow.

A woman like her, with dark hair and eye coloring, would look her best offset by bold fabrics, and she had a body meant for daring styles, low necklines and high hemlines. Instead, everything about Mallory said tentative in a quiet, hesitant voice. Safe. If he could only dress her himself.

Before he let himself go too far down that dead-end road, he stepped into the open and she glanced his way. "Mallory." He nodded.

"Hey." Her smile wavered slightly.

"Ready?"

"As ready as I'll ever be."

"You look nervous."

"I wasn't sure what to wear." She glanced down at her dress. "Do I look okay?"

"You look lovely." He held out his arm and they walked past a row of stores on the way toward the main exit.

She glanced into one of the exclusive shops and sucked in a quiet breath. Curious, he followed her gaze to the halter-style dress in the window. It was as sexy as the one she was wearing was harmless.

For the hell of it, he stopped and nodded toward the mannequin. "Now, in that, you'd be an absolute knockout." The hemline, uneven, chiffon folds falling below the knee, was longer than he would've liked to see on her, but a tight bodice made up for it.

She shook her head. "I don't wear red."

"You are joking. Why not?"

"It's not my style."

How could that be? Red would look perfect with her dark coloring and the style. *Aí.* "Want to make my night?"

"Not particularly." She laughed, but he could see her curiosity had been piqued. "Okay, fine. What would make your night?"

"For you to try on that dress."

She looked at him as if he'd grown another head.

"What are you afraid of?"

"Who said I was afraid?" She stalked into the shop toward the salesperson and pointed to the dress in the window.

Roberto followed, holding back his smile. She was so easy. The clerk found Mallory the correct size, and a few minutes later, she came out of the changing room, looking better than he'd guessed. With her own silver sandals and rhinestone accessories, she looked damned near perfect.

Suddenly, much to his own consternation, the act of *undressing* her was beginning to hold significant appeal. What the hell was this all about? Not only had he given up women as well as meaningless sex more than a year ago, he hadn't once regretted it. Until this very moment.

"What do you think?" she asked uncertainly, studying her reflection in the mirror.

"Amazing." *Espectacular.*

"It's too tight. Too short." She tugged and squiggled.

And she was adorable. "The fabric stretches. It's perfect."

The dress fit snugly through the bodice and cupped her bottom, only to flare out from there in sheer folds. She spun around, and, immediately, he wished he could take her dancing. To see her at the end of his hand, spinning and swinging those gorgeous, full curves.

That was it. He slapped a credit card on the glass counter.

"Wait a minute," she said. "I'm not sure—"

"I am buying it."

"But…I don't know…"

He glanced at the clerk. "*Por favor,* tell her."

The clerk smiled apologetically, as if she were betraying an *amigo.* "You do look stunning. And I'm not just saying that."

Mallory glanced at the price tag. "I can't really afford this."

"I can." He signaled to the clerk, who hesitated. Mallory stood looking at her reflection with a scowl on her face. He stepped behind her, appearing above her head in the mirror. "Let me do this for you."

She studied him, and then, as if making a difficult decision, took a tube of lipstick out of her purse and replaced the neutral color she'd been wearing with a deep red. She turned, dazzling him with her transformation. "Want to make *my* night?" she asked.

"How could I possibly refuse?" The scent of honey tickled his nose, momentarily distracting him. Was that her skin or her hair? The sudden urge to find out hit him hard and he backed away.

"Let's skip dinner and a show."

"In favor of?" His imagination took off and settled on a few interesting alternatives, all of which curiously involved his hotel room and a big bed.

"A casino."

"You want to go to a casino?" He wasn't sure he'd heard correctly.

"Yep. I want to have fun tonight."

"That is not a good idea."

"Since when is fun not a good idea?"

Since it wasn't on Theo and Patricia's agenda. "Look—"

"We're in Las Vegas and I've never been to a casino other than for taping this week. Come on, Roberto. Teach me to gamble. You know you want to." She grinned. "What are you afraid of?"

He glanced down into her face, her eyes guileless and beseeching. How could he refuse such a beautiful woman? "*Querida,* it seems we are a match made in heaven."

CHAPTER FOUR

ROBERTO DROVE UP to the front door of The Palms and hopped out. He handed the keys to the parking attendant and came around to Mallory's side of the car. Camera flashes lit up all around them, and her heart raced.

"Roberto!" a man yelled from where the paparazzi were lined near the entrance.

What the hell had she gotten herself into? How in the world had she come to be sitting in a luxury European convertible, of all things, dressed in a slinky and expensive red number of a dress and heading into a casino to gamble? Of course this had all been her own doing, but the logic that had gotten her to this moment had suddenly and completely deserted her.

"Mallory?" Roberto held out his hand for her. "Are you ready?"

She glanced at him, classy and gorgeous in a black suit and silky shirt, and felt like an impostor. She was out of her league. Way out. She was kidding herself in thinking she could break out of her mold. She was America's Sweetheart for a very good reason. The label fit. Perfectly.

"Come on." He smiled. "This was your idea. Remember?"

Somehow her hand ended up in his, and his touch felt surprisingly warm and reassuring, infusing her with renewed commitment. She was an actress. She could do this. She took a deep breath and climbed out of the convertible.

"That's Mallory Dalton!" someone else said as the cameras clicked away.

"With Roberto Castillo!"

He tucked her hand under his arm and walked toward the

entrance. She caught sight of her reflection in the window and stared. That couldn't be her. That woman looked too pretty, too confident, too poised. The outside was everything she didn't feel on the inside. Oh, but it was such a gorgeous dress.

Of course, her heel decided to, at that exact moment, get caught in a crack on the sidewalk. She stumbled, falling forward. Roberto reacted, throwing his arm in front of her and stopping her fall.

"Thanks." Swallowing, she glanced at him.

"You are trembling," Roberto whispered, holding her arm as they walked through the crowds. "Having second thoughts?"

"Yes."

"I don't bite, you know. I swear."

"That's not what I've heard."

His honest laughter went a long way toward settling her nerves. "Oh, come on. How bad could it be?" He squeezed her hand.

"You're right," she said. "I'm being silly."

"You know, I can't walk into a casino," he said, clearly trying to drum up conversation in the hope of helping her relax, "without thinking of the first time I went to Monte Carlo."

"When was that?"

"Almost ten years ago. I was twenty-one, my career was about to skyrocket and the staff treated me like a young prince. Since then, casinos have been one of my favorite places in the world."

"Why?"

"People are always having a great time." He drew her toward the heart of the casino. "Look around," he said, "at the action. The life happening in every direction."

She watched and listened. Slot machines whirred. People laughed and talked. Dealers and handlers called out across their tables. Roulette wheels spun. Dice rolled. The noise was nearly deafening, but he was right. The place was full of life.

Roberto looked as if he was absorbing every second of it. "This is going to be fun," he said, glancing down at her. "I promise. So you can quit looking as if you are heading off to a firing squad."

"Sorry."

"How do we get you comfortable?" he asked.

That was simple. "Take off this lipstick and this dress. Give me my own jeans and T-shirt. And send me in a cab back to my hotel room."

He looked at her as if he understood the feeling.

"How 'bout a drink?" He stopped at a bar and held out a stool for her.

She'd never been much for alcohol and ordered the first thing that came to her mind. "A margarita, please." The sweet and sour concoction was a standby of her sister Tara's and their old high school buddies. When he asked for a club soda, she threw him a questioning look.

He shrugged. "I don't drink alcohol."

"Ever?" That didn't fit.

"A little more than a year ago, after winning one of the toughest championships of my career, I partied all night long. Woke up in Paris. With no recollection of how I got there."

Now that *did* fit. "Were there women involved?"

For a moment he looked as if he wasn't going to answer. "Two of them," he said without a smile, as if the memory bothered him. "I awoke the next morning with a raging hangover unable to remember either one of their names. It wasn't one of my finer moments."

His honesty surprised her. "Since then, you haven't had any alcohol?"

The bartender delivered their drinks.

"Only my father's wine. Only when I'm home. And only because I wouldn't want to insult him." Still pensive, he turned his glass round and round on the bar.

Deciding a change in subject might not be such a bad idea, she asked, "So your father, he makes his own wine?"

"He tends a small vineyard on some property I own not far out of Buenos Aires. He's always loved the country."

"And you?"

"Always hated it. Ran away to Buenos Aires when I was sixteen." He studied her. "Maybe I'm the reason you can't get comfortable. Then again, I'll bet you have never been comfortable around men, have you?"

Feeling defensive, she took a small sip of margarita and lifted her chin. "Sure I have."

"You have no brothers. Your father's the sweetest man on the planet. And you blushed when you were young."

"Two out of three."

"Which one did I get wrong?"

"I'm not telling." She grinned, noticing for the first time that the more comfortable he got around her, the more pronounced his accent sounded.

"Ah, there we go." He took her hand. "When you smile, all is good."

"You're a shameless flirt."

"I am Argentinean. What can you expect?"

"Arrogant and beautiful." She'd read that somewhere, too.

"Perfecto."

She shook her head. "I can never tell whether or not you're serious."

"Most people can't."

"Are you ever serious?"

"Rarely." He gazed directly into her eyes. "Unless I'm on a racetrack."

"So why flirt, then, if you don't always mean it?"

The question seemed to surprise him. "To get a woman in bed. Why else?"

"Most women would happily jump into your bed without a single word."

He laughed. "Not you. You have already made that crystal clear."

"There's more to it than that." She waited.

He went back to spinning his glass. "I suppose flirting is what people expect from me," he said. "And it comes easily. I learned from one of the best."

"Your father."

He nodded. "A hopeless romantic."

"How did your mother stand it?"

"She didn't." Roberto looked away. "I didn't meet her until I was sixteen."

"I'm sorry."

"Don't be. Her slamming the door in my face was probably the best thing that could have happened to me."

"What?" Already, Mallory hated the woman. "How could her rejection have been good?"

"I'd run away from my father's home, so I couldn't go back. Still, I had to eat. Took a job as a janitor and then a mechanic at the local racetrack and was discovered several months later. One thing led to another and before I knew it, I was racing open-wheel. And winning." He glanced down at her barely touched margarita. "Are you going to drink that or not?"

"I don't know why I ordered it." She shrugged.

"Come on. Let's have some fun." He tucked her hand around his arm. "Blackjack?"

"You play. I'll watch."

"*Aí*. No. The deal was I teach you to gamble, remember?" He looked around for a table and sat her down in front of him. "It's easy. You can't go wrong if you follow the rules."

"Okay," she said tentatively.

"Don't worry. I'll tell you what to do."

She swallowed and drew several hundred dollars out of her purse.

"Put that away." He tucked her money back in her hand. "If you lose I don't want it on my head."

"If I win?"

He grinned. "My stake, my take." He threw several thousand dollars onto the table and the dealer put a stack of chips in front of Mallory. She went to pick them up and knocked several off the table.

Roberto caught the chips in midair.

She glanced into his eyes. "You're awfully fast."

"That's what all the women say."

"Seriously. Your reflexes."

"Some of it's natural," he said, shrugging it off. "But I train. Constantly." He stacked the chips in front of her.

"That's a lot of money."

"Don't worry about it." He rested his hands on her shoulders and squeezed. "Tonight, money's no concern. Throw in a chip."

Mallory followed his directions. In the span of a few minutes, she was down several thousand dollars. Maybe she shouldn't have suggested this. "Do you know what you're doing?" she asked.

The sound of his laughter thrummed through her. "*Querida,* I have logged more than my share of time at blackjack tables," he said. "But you go right ahead. Do your own thing, if you'd like."

For the next several hands, he didn't offer any advice. She lost every time, despite feeling as if she was beginning to understand the rules. "This isn't my game," she said. "Maybe we should cut our losses and move on."

"Just when you are getting warmed up?" He tossed a few more thousand onto the table. On the next hand, she was dealt two eights. "Split your cards."

"What?"

He explained the rule, the odds, the reason. "That makes sense." She won both hands. "This is crazy." She shook her head, but had to admit she felt more than a little giddy inside. "Winning's a heck of a lot more fun than losing."

"Oh, I don't know. Win or lose. We are here to be entertained, right?" He showed her how to double down and, before they knew it, the dealer was setting several thousand dollars worth of chips in front of her.

"Woo hoo!" She spun toward him and grabbed his arm. "My luck is turning."

"You think so, huh?" His expression turned serious. "Looks like you have blackjack down." He set several chips down for a dealer tip and then backed away from the table. "Let's see how you do at craps."

As they stood, Roberto reached around Mallory and directed her through the casino. Though the gesture was meant to be as natural and impersonal as a handshake, there was something comforting about the warmth of his hand low on her back that had her moving closer toward him. Suddenly, he spun her around just before a camera flashed behind him.

Over his shoulder, Roberto glared at the photographer. "Take off or I'll call security."

The man shrugged and walked away.

"What's the big deal?" she asked.

"We are supposed to be at a nice quiet dinner and a show, remember? What would America think of their favorite sweetheart in one of Sin City's biggest casinos?"

Dammit. That had been exactly her point.

"I can't believe this is your first time in a casino." He looked down at her. "How old are you, anyway?"

"Thirty."

He threw back his head and laughed out loud.

She couldn't help but smile along with him.

"You are not," he said.

"Am, too."

"Not."

She whipped out her driver's license.

"Huh. Well then, I'd say it's about time someone corrupted you. Let's teach you how to play craps." He handed her back her driver's license and glanced around for a table. "I'll place the bets. You can be the shooter."

"So I roll the dice?"

"*Perfecto.* That's all you have to do." He steered her toward a group of people standing around an oval table yelling excitedly. Leaning toward her, he whispered again in her ear. "When the shooter rolls a seven, his turn rolling the dice will be over, they'll flip over those markers from white to black. Then you can take a turn."

He positioned her clockwise from the current shooter. She watched the table, listened to them calling and yelling. Roberto stood directly behind her. His heat penetrated the thin fabric of her dress, at once setting her at ease and heightening her awareness. She had to admit, she felt damned sexy in this filmy, flirty fabric.

Soon, a crowd gathered, pushing in behind them and forcing them closer together. Quite unexpectedly, his hands rested on her upper arms. She stiffened. It was all she could do not to let herself fall back against him. *This isn't real,* she reminded herself. *Not real at all.*

"You're enjoying this, aren't you?" she said. "Making me uncomfortable."

"Is that what I'm doing?"

"Yes."

"Then I suppose I am getting a kick out of it."

She could almost hear him grinning and elbowed him.

He only chuckled and moved closer. "Pay attention now," he whispered in her ear. As two dealers, one at each end of the table, paid the winners, he gave her a brief rundown on the rules. "It's all odds, *querida.* That's all there is to it."

The dealers flipped the pucks to black, notifying everyone a new game would be starting. Roberto exchanged several thousand dollars for chips, placed a few on something called the pass line and said, "Your turn to roll. Use one hand, don't rub them together and try to bounce them off the other end of the table."

She grabbed the dice.

"Throw me a seven or eleven," he said, explaining those were the most likely numbers to be rolled. "Seven or eleven."

She threw the dice. Seven. Everyone around the table seemed to win. After the dealers paid those with chips on the table, Roberto took his winnings. "Try again. Seven or eleven."

Fascinated, Mallory watched as one of the dealers used a stick to move the dice in front of her. She threw them again and rolled another seven. "Yes!" she yelled.

Every time she picked up the dice, a thrill of anticipation ran through her. It seemed all she could roll were sevens or elevens, and the gamblers around the table were shouting with excitement. Roberto let some of his winnings ride and, despite heavily tipping the dealers at the table, they amassed quite a long row of chips in front of Mallory.

Finally her streak ended and she threw a six. "Is that okay?" she asked.

"It's good." Roberto placed stacks of chips on the table and called out bets to the dealers.

When he began explaining what he was doing, Mallory waved her hand. "Just tell me what to roll."

"Now, anything *except* a seven."

People were gathering around the table, placing bets, crossing their fingers, whispering the numbers they wanted. She felt their excitement, their expectation. They were looking at her as if she were the queen of the casino, and she loved it. She stretched her shoulders, blew a kiss onto the dice and tossed them across the table.

"Hard eight," the dealer announced the roll.

Shouts erupted around the table as Roberto laughed. Apparently that was a big deal because the dealer set a large stack of chips in front of them. The gamblers placed more frantic bets around the table.

Mallory jumped up and down. She could get used to this.

"You are on a roll." Roberto laughed. "I should feel guilty for turning you into a gambler, but I'm having too much fun watching you."

Mallory's grin widened as she watched everyone around the table place their bets. "Now what?"

He set another handful of chips on various spots on the table. "Roll anything but a seven. I don't care. We are out for a good time, right?"

She kept winning. And winning. Roll after roll after roll. The table turned frantic with activity. People around the table yelled out all kinds of different bets to the dealers, but none of it made any sense to Mallory. Roberto, on the other hand, was down to placing only one or two bets.

"Is something wrong?" she asked.

"Getting tired." He hid a yawn behind his hand. "It's been a long day."

"Do you want me to quit?" she asked, purely out of politeness.

"And risk being pummeled by everyone at this table for taking away their lucky charm?" He chuckled as if he could tell by looking at her that she wasn't quite ready to leave the casino. "I think not. Roll 'em again, *querida*."

After a few more tosses, she rolled a seven and ended her long-running streak. The whole table groaned, but nodded their appreciation, for the stacks of chips in front of each person had grown substantially.

The man on her left took his turn rolling and Roberto leaned in to teach her how to place a few simple bets. After a few turns, she was betting odds on the pass line and placing her own proposition, field and hard way bets. And winning.

Roberto whispered in her ear, "I think we should go." He sounded agitated.

She glanced back to find him glaring past the other side of the table. That same photographer was back, this time less than twenty feet away and working a corner slot machine.

"I don't care if he gets a picture," she said. In fact, she could only *hope* he did. "I'm having fun."

"Mallory, don't push it. Let's go. *My* agent I can handle, but I'm going to guess Theo will hit the roof if he finds out I took you to a casino."

"All right, fine." She hadn't considered how her actions might get Roberto into trouble. "But for the record, you're the killjoy tonight."

They cashed in their chips and Roberto had netted significant winnings. "I think I'd better bring you along every time I go gambling." Smiling, he took her hand, and they headed back to her hotel. After pulling up to the main entrance, he hopped out of the sports car and walked her into the lobby.

Near the elevators, she faltered. No matter how sexy he looked, this wasn't a real date. That meant no real kiss.

He glanced at her lips as if his thoughts were tracking right behind hers. "I had a nice time tonight," he said.

"You sound surprised."

"I am, actually." He grinned. "Our agents scheduled you to come to the race on Sunday."

"Is that okay with you?"

He nodded, studying her. "I'll send a driver with instructions to bring you right into the infield. Would you like to sit on the war wagon?"

On pit road? *Um, yeah.* "With Harry Skelly? And the rest of your team?"

He nodded.

"I'd love it." An awkward silence hung between them. "So now what?"

Without touching her, he whispered, "You could invite me to your room."

Yes, she could, and it'd probably be a hell of a good time. But then what? She studied his eyes, looking for some indication as to whether he really wanted her, or if this was simply the logical outcome for the evening. His deep brown eyes were unreadable, and if Theo got wind of Roberto spending the night, he'd call off this deal so fast all their heads would be spinning, and then her plan would fall apart.

"That's the only bad idea you've had all night," she said.

"What did you expect from a bad boy?"

She'd been right. "And what response did *you* expect from a good girl?"

"I knew there was a reason I like bad girls."

"And look where it's gotten you."

"Touché." Grinning, he turned toward the exit. "I'll make sure the paparazzi see me heading back to my own hotel."

"Good idea." She didn't want to smash her sweetheart mold with a sledgehammer. A nice, steady picking action would work best. She stepped into the elevator and breathed a sigh of relief when the doors closed, leaving her blessedly alone.

This game they were both playing was dangerous. One of them was going to win and the other lose. All Mallory could hope for was a little beginner's luck.

CHAPTER FIVE

"CRAPS WAS DEFINITELY NOT on last night's agenda." Patricia slapped the newspaper down on the table in front of Roberto.

Sitting in his hotel room and eating breakfast Saturday morning before he headed out to the track for practice, Roberto scooped up a forkful of eggs, shoved them into his mouth and glanced down at the paper. Two photos were displayed side by side. The first depicted Kacy slapping him and the second showed Mallory and him together at the casino.

He had no clue when the photographer had snapped the picture, but the man had managed to get a good one. Mallory was in front of him, and he was very close behind her with his hands on her upper arms. Even now, he could almost smell the sweet scent of honey and envision her bare shoulders. Her skin, a natural tan tint, had felt soft and supple, like the finest of cashmere.

And then he read the heading over the pictures: Taming The Ultimate Bad Boy? And the subhead: Can Mallory Dalton Accomplish What Kacy Haughton Couldn't?

There was no help for it. He laughed out loud. "I'd say this is exactly the outcome you and Theo Stein had hoped for, Patricia."

"That's not the point." Patricia poured herself a cup of coffee and sat down across from him.

"Then what is?"

"Theo woke me this morning screaming into the phone. He said that if something like this happens again, then the deal is off."

Agents. Roberto hoped to hell Stein hadn't read the riot act to Mallory. That would really piss him off.

"Did you two even make it to the restaurant last night?" Patricia asked. "The show?"

"No." And he'd be damned if he'd regret it.

He flashed on how perfect Mallory had looked dressed in red and sitting in his bright yellow convertible. He'd been tempted to buy the rental car for her because for the first time in a long while, he'd actually had some decent fun going out with a woman. With a vigilance he'd rarely noticed in the opposite sex, she'd listened to his directions last night, followed the dealers and studied how the other players were betting. In no time, she'd been betting on her own, winning and having a damned good time.

Maybe innocent didn't necessarily equate to boring, at least not where Mallory was concerned.

"Why not?" Patricia wasn't going to let it go.

"Because Mallory wanted to go to a casino."

"Liar."

He laughed again. In truth, he couldn't blame Patricia. Mallory had surprised him, too. What a disarming little nymph she'd been, a complete contradiction, with her wide, almost wicked smile and uncertain twinkle in her eyes. He wondered if their sweet Mallory Dalton didn't hide quite a wide streak of bad under her good-girl skin.

"You win. It was my fault." He finished the rest of his breakfast and stood, wanting nothing more than his car, a long stretch of track and some good runs.

"Roberto, this is going to be an extremely delicate situation. If we're not careful, this whole thing could backfire on us."

"You mean on me."

"You could end up looking as if you're corrupting America's Sweetheart."

"I'm only a lowly man, Patricia. Not very good at games."

"That's why you need to do what I'm telling you from here on out. Agreed?"

"Whatever." He grabbed his duffel bag.

"She's coming to the race tomorrow, right?"

He nodded and took a deep breath. It'd been a long time since he'd invited any woman other than his mother to see one of his races. What the hell had come over him, asking Mallory to pit road? Then he remembered the excitement on her face. Entertaining her had been so easy, so fun. He wondered what her bedroom smile would look like.

"Yeah, she'll be there. I asked her to sit on the war wagon."

"Really?"

"I figured it'd make you and the Grossos happy." That part of the game he understood. "The TV crews are bound to get a few clips of her."

Patricia narrowed her eyes at him. "Keep your cool tomorrow and don't scare her off, okay?"

He headed toward the door. "Mallory can take care of herself, Patricia." He had the feeling she was a lot tougher than most people realized.

"It's important you remember something." When he turned back around, Patricia pierced him with her clear and focused gaze. "You need Mallory Dalton far more than she needs you."

"ARE YOU out of your mind?" Shirley Dalton's voice had taken on a high-pitched, erratic sound. "Being with that man on the show is one thing. Benign. Safe. With all those people around. But a date?"

"I don't get it," Mallory said, exhausted. "You and Dad are such big NASCAR fans, I would've guessed you'd be excited to find out I went out with Roberto."

Mallory slipped off her flip-flops, stretched her legs out on the hotel bed and leaned back against the pillows. It was late Saturday evening, and she'd only now gotten back to her room. The *Racing Hearts* director had wanted to wrap up the on-location shots in Las Vegas, so the cast and crew had put in overtime to make it happen. After leaving the set a short time ago, Mallory had opened her cell phone to find eight unread messages, all of them from her mom, dad and two sisters, Tara and Emma-Lee.

"Couldn't you have found someone," her mother went on, "not quite so…so wild? Someone more like Tara's Adam? Roberto Castillo doesn't have a very…nice reputation."

Nice? Mallory smiled to herself. No, she'd never describe Roberto as *nice.* "My agent thinks being seen with him is a smart move for my career."

"Career? Sweetheart, I'm not talkin' about your job," her mother went on. "This is about you…your…"

Virginity? Mallory almost laughed out loud. Did her mother seriously think that, at thirty, her oldest daughter had never slept with a man? Come to think of it, she probably did. And Mallory couldn't very well blame her. She'd never been the type to spill details about her few-and-far-between relationships with men through the years.

"Mom, it was a simple date. One date." That might have ended with him coming to her room. If he'd asked one more time, if he'd kissed her, if he'd tried to persuade her, she would've been a goner.

"I can't imagine any date with a man like Roberto Castillo being the least bit simple. Were you alone with him?"

"Mom…" Mallory said. "I—"

"Hold on. Your father wants to talk with you."

Oh God. They were going to pass her back and forth like a tennis ball. One thing she could say about her parents: they always backed each other up.

Tara and Emma-Lee, too, had probably come home for the weekend, to the house they'd all grown up in outside of Mooresville. Mallory could easily imagine all four of them gathered in the newly updated blue-and-white kitchen discussing the eldest Dalton's misfit life. No doubt, they'd each have their own suggestions for mapping out her next several years.

She couldn't really blame them. Throughout most of her childhood, Mallory had never seemed to have much direction in her life. College had lasted for only one semester before she'd about died of boredom from all those general eds. And the next few years had turned into a succession of one job after another. She'd worked at everything from telemarketing to real estate and had hated every single job.

Then, around ten years ago, when she'd first left North Carolina for New York City, they'd assumed it was another whim and had been filled with cautionary and alternative advice. *You shouldn't do this. You should do that. You can't do this. You can do that. It's dangerous. It's expensive. It's unnecessary. Come home. Come home. Come home.*

As if moving to a big city hadn't been frightening enough for a small-town Southern girl, every step she'd taken had felt weighted in cement. She'd been thrilled and excited for her life to finally begin. The opportunity to go out into the world and *be* something, anything, had finally been at hand.

"Mary-Jean, you there?" her father said. "Mary-Jean."

Ten years since she'd changed her name to Mallory, and her parents still called her Mary-Jean. She was sure they didn't mean to hurt her feelings. They simply didn't understand.

"Hi, Dad. Yes, I'm here."

"Have you seen a paper today? Or the entertainment news?"

No, she hadn't. After the late night out, she'd slept until the very last minute and rushed out the door to make it to the set on time. Besides, she'd made up her mind there was no point in micromanaging this deal. Getting her desired results over time was all that mattered. "Why are you so upset?"

"Because…well…it's just that…" Mallory's father sputtered over the phone line. "I couldn't believe my eyes when I saw that picture of you with Roberto Castillo. When did you learn to play craps and what in God's name are you doin' in Vegas?"

She smiled, thinking about how she'd enjoyed last night, feeling Roberto's warmth right behind her, his breath on her neck, his voice in her ear. She hadn't had that much fun in…heck, she'd never had that much fun.

"Mary-Jean? You listening to me?"

"Sorry, Dad. We're here this week filming for the show. And I was having a good time at the casino last night."

"The paper says you're Roberto's new girlfriend. That you caused a breakup between him and another woman. That happened mighty fast."

"You can't believe everything you see in the paper."

"Roberto Castillo's not…well, he's got quite a reputation for being a ladies' man, Mary-Jean. We raised you to be a good girl. That man…he's…"

"Oh, for heaven's sake, Buddy." Mallory heard her mother's voice in the background. "Give me back that phone." There was a pause on the line, and then, "Sometimes, I think I don't know you anymore, Mary-Jean. You should move back home, quit that acting job. That lifestyle's not good for you. New York is turning you into a different person."

Maybe that wasn't such a bad thing. She really hadn't understood Mary-Jean Dalton. Mallory Dalton, on the other hand, was finally making sense, and she was fed up with her family thinking they could direct her life.

"Mallory?" Now Tara was on the line.

"Hi, Tara."

"That man's going to chew you up and spit you out," she said. "You know he will."

"No, I don't know that. Will you please put me on speakerphone? I have something to say, and I want to say it only once. To everyone."

"All right," Tara said. "You're on speaker."

"Is Emma-Lee there, too?"

"Hi, Mallory." Emma was the youngest of the three Dalton sisters. "Personally, I think Roberto's hot! Way to go, girl!"

"Emma-Lee," their father cautioned.

"That's enough," said their mother.

"Okay. Here's the deal." Mallory took a deep breath. She couldn't tell them the whole truth. Bless her parents' hearts, but they couldn't keep a secret to save their souls. "Roberto Castillo and I are friends. That's all."

"Men like that don't have friends, Mary-Jean." That was her dad. "No matter what he's told you."

"Honey, what if all he wants is a quick affair? Then what?" That, from her mom.

"I appreciate all of your concerns. But…" She hesitated. How did one go about breaking thirty-year-old patterns? "I think I know what I'm doing."

"Okay, okay." That was Tara's voice. "I'm going to talk to her in private." After a few minutes and some muffled noises, Mallory's sister came back on the line. "I took you off speaker, and I'm in my old bedroom. Tell me what's really going on."

"You can't say anything to anyone, especially not Mom and Dad. And not Adam, either." Knowing Tara, she probably told her fiancé everything.

"Can I tell Emma?"

"Yes, but you have to make her promise to keep it a secret first."

"Okay. Shoot."

"Roberto and I have an arrangement."

Tara chuckled. "That's sounds kinda kinky."

"Not even close. This is a public relations deal to help him clean up his public image for NASCAR fans and the Grossos."

"And he's using you to do that." Tara sighed. "What do you get out of it?"

"He's a high-profile driver. The more publicity I get, the better my chances of getting the lead in that movie, *Three Sisters,* that I told you about. They'll be taking auditions soon."

"What makes you think an association with him won't damage your image? This could very well backfire on you."

"Maybe I don't like being America's Sweetheart anymore. Maybe it's time for a change."

"Hmm. What about him and Kacy Haughton?"

"He said they were finished months ago."

"Not sure I'd believe that, but where'd you get that gorgeous red dress?"

"Roberto bought it for me."

The phone line went silent for a moment. "You're playing with fire, big sis," Tara whispered. "Your career might be able to handle the heat, but I not sure there's enough insulation around your heart."

CHAPTER SIX

"I CAN'T DECIDE whether you're an idiot," said Dean Grosso, Roberto's new employer, tossing a newspaper on the hood of Roberto's No. 507 car, "or a genius."

Roberto and his crew chief, Harry Skelly, had been discussing changes required to his car's setup in the relative coolness of the garage stall at the Las Vegas track. Roberto had placed an adequate fifteenth in qualifying and was now making some practice runs around the track to determine final adjustments.

Together, he and Harry glanced down at the pictures on the paper, the same ones with him, Kacy and Mallory that Patricia had previously shown him.

"If you were winning races," Dean said, "I probably wouldn't give a hoot what you do with your spare time. But since you're not even placing in the Top Ten, this is the extent of the news the American public gets to read about you."

When Patsy Grosso came to stand next to her husband with her arms crossed in front of her, Harry took it as his cue to leave.

"Hello, Patsy," Roberto said.

Her answering smile was tolerant, at best.

When Nathan Cargill, dressed impeccably, as always, in a white shirt and gray pants, joined the Grossos, Roberto felt well out-numbered.

"Nathan."

"Roberto." Nathan nodded, but kept his distance. While the man had agreed, after the murder of his father last December, to operate as acting team manager until the Grossos felt comfortable running Cargill-Grosso Racing on their own, Nathan had clearly been distracted lately. He seemed to want to turn over the reins as quickly as possible.

"Look," Roberto said. "We—"

"Figure it out, okay?" Dean interrupted. "Our agreement was you were to clean up your image, and we're going to hold you to it. Honestly, Patsy and I have enough other things to worry about without having to concern ourselves with our new driver's love life."

Roberto had heard about the Grossos hiring a private investigator to find their missing child, Gina, their son Kent's twin sister who'd been kidnapped at birth. An anonymous blogger claimed Gina hadn't died as the FBI had concluded three decades ago. That had to be weighing heavily on the couple. And, as if that wasn't enough, they had their daughter Sophia's wedding coming up in April.

"I'm sorry, Dean," Roberto said. "I didn't mean to add to your troubles."

Dean shook his head. "When Patricia ran her idea about cameo appearances in *Racing Hearts* by us, we thought it was a great idea. But dating Mallory Dalton? That's taking things a step too far if you ask me."

"We all met her at the NASCAR Awards Banquet," Patsy said. "She's very sweet."

"Yes, she is, but we are not dating."

"You're not?" Patsy asked.

"No. Patricia took the *Racing Hearts* cameo idea one step further and concocted a plan with Mallory's agent to get us together. It's only for publicity's sake."

"Well, in that case," Nathan said, "maybe you're not such an idiot after all. She may very well have helped you weather this Kacy storm."

"I imagine that was the idea," Patsy said, concern furrowing her brow. "The question is, now what? You can't control the media."

"Mallory's coming to the race tomorrow." He paused. "I asked her to sit with Harry."

"Sounds like trouble to me." Dean shook his head. "I want you focusing on tomorrow's race. Not some woman. And while you're at it, try to remember the No. 414 car is your teammate, not your competition."

Roberto nodded at the reference to Dean's son, Kent. "I'm working on it."

"Why aren't you staying in a motor home in the drivers' lot this weekend?"

Roberto shook his head. No way was he trading in penthouse suites and room service for a slideout bedroom and backyard barbecues.

"We'll get you one of these days."

Patsy stayed back as Dean and Nathan walked away. "Is Mallory fully aware of the details of this dating deal?" she asked.

"Yes, ma'am."

"And she's going along with it?"

Roberto nodded.

"Well, regardless of what Dean and Nathan think," Patsy said, tucking a strand of hair behind her ear, "I want you to remember that Mallory Dalton's a living, breathing person. Not a marketing tool."

MALLORY WAS LATE. Late, late, late.

The car Roberto had sent to take her to the track had been waiting outside the hotel for nearly half an hour. She'd overslept, taken too long in the shower and couldn't for the life of her decide what to wear.

She'd watched enough NASCAR races to know that the cameramen tended to show brief clips of the drivers' wives or girlfriends throughout the long races. With Roberto requesting she hang out with his team in the pit stall, there was a big chance she could be on national TV in front of something like eight million viewers. If ever there was a time to panic, this was it.

This is a role, she kept telling herself as she flipped through her closet, discarding one outfit choice after another. *No different than Racing Hearts.*

Finally, she settled on jeans and a white T-shirt and hoped she didn't spill anything on herself. It was safe, and she'd never been comfortable sticking out.

She raced out of the hotel, found the driver Roberto had sent and settled into the car's backseat. A short time later, the driver brought her right to the security gates, handed her credentials for the day and found an attendant with a golf cart to take her to Roberto's garage. Years and years ago, Mallory had visited infields with her parents, but this was an entirely different experience. She felt like royalty.

Roberto's red-and-white No. 507 car was parked outside one of the garage stalls and she held her breath, searching the area for Roberto. When she found him amidst a group of his team members, dressed in his Molloy Cycles uniform and wearing wraparound sunglasses, her heart pitter-pattered. He was as sexy in his red-and-white uniform as he'd been the other night in a black suit and silk shirt.

He glanced up, caught her eye and immediately separated himself from the other men gathered near his car. "Hey, there." He reached for her hand and thanked the cart driver. "I was beginning to think you chickened out."

She couldn't seem to find any words.

"Nervous? Again?"

She swallowed. "You have no idea."

For a heart-stopping minute, he looked as if he was considering kissing her. When he put a fingertip to her lips, the motion, combined with the intensity in his gaze, was almost more intimate than a kiss. "Come on," he said instead. "Meet the guys."

He introduced her to all of his team members, but there was little chance she'd remember all their names. Between the jackman, the gasman, the tire changers, the tire carriers, the spotter and the rest of the team, there were too many of them. Harry Skelly, his crew chief, she recognized from his years racing in NASCAR.

"You're welcome to sit on the war wagon with me," Harry said. "I could use the company."

"Thank you." She smiled. "I'd love to."

"If you are going to sit on pit road, *querida,* you need our team colors," Roberto said, drawing her into their hauler parked behind their garage. "The sun's pretty hot out there. How 'bout a hat?" He grabbed a baseball cap from a cabinet and held it toward her.

"Sounds good."

"A Molloy Cycles T-shirt?"

Red, like her dress Friday night.

"You already know you'll look good in it." He pointed toward the back of the hauler. "If you want, you can change."

She found the small bathroom, changed shirts and gathered her hair into a ponytail and pulled it through the back of the cap. A glance in the mirror caught her by surprise. Her skin practically glowed and the color of the hat around her face brought out the rich mahogany of her eyes.

Roberto was waiting outside the door. "You look as good in that getup as you did the other night."

"Always flirting."

"No. That's the truth."

"Right."

The next hour or so went by in a haze. She stayed out of the way, but there were several times Roberto brought her back into the fray. He drew her next to him when NSN's reporter, Payton Reese, interviewed him before the race. He held her hand during the team's prerace prayers. Several times, Mallory actually pinched herself to make sure she wasn't dreaming.

Before she knew it, she was sitting next to Harry on the war wagon with a headset on watching the race on a monitor. She couldn't speak to Roberto, but she could listen to everything he, Harry and their spotter said to each other. She found herself rooting for Roberto, for their team, and every time he hit pit road, he glanced up at her. For a woman who had cut her teeth on racing, this was as close to heaven as it got.

"Twenty to go," Roberto's spotter said.

If he could maintain, this would be his best finish yet. He'd led for a few laps and had stayed within the top ten cars for a good portion of the race. Then the steering wheel shook and jerked right. *"Maldito sea,"* he yelled, words flowing like rapid fire from his mouth. *"Algo pasó con mi neumático."*

"Whoa, whoa," Harry said. "Stay loose. I can't understand anything you're saying."

Then Roberto's front tire blew and he ended up riding the outside wall.

"You're clear," Harry said. "No one's gonna hit you."

"I'm coming in."

"Caution's up."

He pulled into his pit box and glanced up while they were changing all four tires. Mallory looked down at him, but, behind those dark sunglasses, it was hard reading her expression. Or maybe he was distracted by the race. Or was she distracting him from the race? Hell, he couldn't tell.

"Go, go, go." They finished changing his tires, and he headed back out on the track.

He'd fallen back to thirty-first. Dammit. This could have been his best showing and then he'd had to go and blow a tire.

"Focus, Roberto," Harry said.

Focus on what?

"Kent could use some help," Harry said. "Can you move up a spot or two?"

"For Kent, or for me?" he said, getting angry.

"I can't understand you when you get excited," Harry said. "What did you say?"

"I said am I moving for Kent or for me?"

"You're on the same team, Roberto. Remember that."

He passed the No. 429 car, Trent Matheson, who'd been having trouble all day. Passed another car. And another.

"Doing good," Harry said.

Three wide, Roberto passed the next two cars.

"Stay cool, buddy boy. Five to go."

Justin Murphy was next, but he wasn't giving Roberto an inch.

Five laps left. On the outside, Roberto made his move and passed Justin. Now he was behind Kent.

"Stay loose. You two work together," Harry said. "Okay, buddy boy?"

"I want to pass."

"You do that and you open the door for Murphy to get by both of you."

Roberto ignored Harry, saw his opportunity and pushed past Kent. What he didn't see was Justin Murphy on his tail, coming right behind. They both passed Kent. Checkered flag. The race was over. Roberto had a twenty-third place finish, but his move had pushed Kent back to twenty-fifth.

Roberto got back to the garage and Kent was waiting for him when he hopped out of his car. Mallory, Harry and the rest of his Molloy Cycles team had already made it back from pit road. Several of the guys stepped in front of Kent as if getting ready to hold him back.

"I don't know what the hell you're doing out there, but I've got a news flash for you. This isn't open-wheel racing." Kent took a threatening step toward Roberto. If he got one quarter of an inch closer, Roberto was going to punch his lights out.

"I saw an opening and I took it."

"Whether you like it or not," Kent went on, "you're part of a team. Start driving like it!" He spun around and strode off toward his own hauler.

Roberto's team dispersed, and he was surprised to find that Mallory hadn't taken cover. Most of the women he knew would've hightailed it out of there at the first raised voice.

"You'll get the hang of it," she said.

And most women wouldn't have the guts to say anything to him when he was in this kind of mood. "Maybe I should have retired. Like everyone said."

"You're a good driver." She stepped toward him. "Give it time."

She was too decent a person for him. "You don't know what's good for you, do you?" He didn't know where this surge of anger had come from, but he might as well take advantage of it.

"What do you mean?"

He walked into the garage, grabbed the newspaper that Dean

had brought over yesterday with the pictures of him with both Kacy and Mallory and slapped it in her hands.

Coming out of left field, it took her a moment to make sense of the photos. When reality hit, the softness left her face. Good. That was the reaction he'd hoped for.

"So this is why my parents were so upset last night," she murmured and then glared at him. "This photo of you and Kacy was taken at the Bellagio. When? I want to know when."

"The morning I met you."

"So you are still seeing her?"

"No. But maybe I will again, maybe I won't." He was being a bastard and he didn't care. She shouldn't want anything to do with him. "At best I'll disappoint you. At worst…break your heart." Roberto dropped his hands to his sides. "You shouldn't be seeing me. For real or not."

She paced back and forth. A battle raged inside her as clear as the creases worrying her brow. Finally, she stopped in front of him. "Shoulds. Shouldn'ts. Do's. Don'ts." She stepped closer. "I'm sick of playing by the rules. They haven't done me any good so far."

"You are only asking for trouble, Mallory."

"Maybe. But that's my business, isn't it?"

"So what are you proposing? It's obvious that your association with me isn't going to have the planned outcome."

"How 'bout an adjustment to our…arrangement?"

"Such as?"

"My *sweetheart* reputation can probably take a hit from Kacy Haughton, but all it'll take is for you to be seen with one other woman, no matter how innocent the setting, and this all turns into Mallory being played. Poor Mallory. She's too naive. Never saw it coming. I don't want to be anyone's fool."

"Like I said. Get out while you can."

"I have a better idea," she said. "You agree to a couple simple conditions."

He may have, indeed, met his match. "I'm listening."

"First, you get your hair cut."

"What would that prove?"

"That I've put my sweetheart mark on you," she said.

He had other ideas, and they would definitely be a hell of a lot more fun.

"Well?" she said.

"Not going to happen."

"Well, then, you have to at least clean up your act. Try trading the T-shirts and faded jeans for suits."

"I'll think about it."

"Fine." She glared at him. "But this last one's nonnegotiable, and I mean it."

He couldn't wait.

"From this moment on, our arrangement must be exclusive."

"Meaning I see no other women."

"You got it. I will not be made the brunt of jokes in the press. You don't even look at another woman when you're with me, and when you're not with me, you're a saint."

It wouldn't be as hard for him as she thought, but she didn't have to know that. "I'm not sure that's possible."

"Can you do it or not?"

He could walk away from Mallory and claim that she'd called the whole deal off after seeing the photo of him with Kacy. He could get back to focusing on his driving and screw all this publicity. He could, but he didn't want to.

He thought of the way she'd looked in that dress the other night, tossing the dice across the craps table. For the first time in a very long year, he actually wanted a woman. Wanted her in his arms, in his bed. Hell, he hadn't kissed her yet.

"Well?" she asked.

"Deal."

"You sure?"

"A saint it is," he said. "I can already feel the halo forming."

CHAPTER SEVEN

MALLORY SHUT OFF the vacuum cleaner and the sound of her cell phone ringing immediately filled the air. Having been scheduled for the afternoon shoot at the *Racing Hearts* midtown Manhattan studio, she'd decided this morning was a good time to give her Chelsea apartment a thorough cleaning.

She snatched the phone from her purse on the kitchen counter. "Hello."

"Mallory. It's Theo."

Despite the sun streaming through the windows of the high-ceiling loft, her spirits nose-dived. She'd been thrilled when this big-name agent had *discovered* her and made an offer of representation, but, lately, she couldn't help but feel as if the sparkle of their client-agent relationship had completely worn away. Still, he'd done so much for her through the years. Signing on with a different agent would seem like such a betrayal.

"Hi, Theo."

"One picture is worth a thousand lies. Isn't that what they say?"

"What are you talking about?"

"You and Roberto at the Atlanta and Bristol tracks these past couple weeks. Haven't you seen the press?"

Not since the photos of him with Kacy.

"They've been plastered across the entertainment rags. You two even look as if you're holding hands in one shot." His short bark of laughter sounded harsh over the phone line. "If I didn't know better, I'd think you and Roberto were the real thing. He should turn in his driving gloves for an acting job."

The comment stung. She'd actually enjoyed Roberto's company and she'd hoped the feeling was mutual. "So what's the buzz? Good? Bad?"

"All over the board. People don't know what to think of you two together. Some predict you'll be a good influence on him. Others insist he'll turn you to the dark side. Even bad press can be better than no press, but we're still treading a fine line here and need to be careful." He paused. "Maybe you two should see more of each other."

That was going to be a trick. With the filming of *Racing Hearts* split between the midtown Manhattan studio and occasional on-location shoots in Charlotte and Roberto's hectic schedule, the only time they'd been able to schedule together had been on the weekends.

In between times, as far as she knew, Roberto hadn't so much as looked at other women. She'd surprised herself with that sudden burst of bravado back in Vegas when she'd told him their arrangement had to be exclusive. But when she was around him, she felt like a different person. He seemed to bring out the worst in her. Or was it the best?

"Are you sure you can't make the Martinsville race?" Theo's voice held a hint of subtle pressure.

"Positive. We'll be taping all day Saturday."

"You could fly out Sunday morning. Roberto's agent said they'd make his private jet available."

More like Theo had insisted on the jet for his client. "That's very nice, Theo, but I could use a day off. Besides, I'll be in Charlotte first thing next week for his second cameo appearance."

"Oh, good. You can go out with him then. Be visible. Maybe I should make some reservations at a few restaurants."

"Well…" she said, hesitating. "I'll be spending some time with my family, so I'm not sure what my schedule will be like—"

"We can work around that."

"Theo." She had to do this. "I think it's best if I take care of this myself."

There was a short period of awkward silence, and then he said, "All right. Let me know how things go."

"I'll do that."

"By the way, the romantic-comedy audition is lined up."

Dammit. "You know, Theo, I'm fine with doing it, but I'd like something a little meatier next time."

"Sweetheart, we've talked about this until we're both blue in the face. That recovering-drug-addict part is not right for you. It's too far out there. I'm all for expanding your range, but there's no point in shocking your audience. Let's move slowly. Okay? A romantic comedy is a nice steppingstone for America's Sweetheart. *Three Sisters* is an indie flick and pays almost nothing. This comedy keeps you on a track with a major studio. And that's where the money is."

Theo was like a brick wall. He had his way of doing things and that was that. Well, Mallory wasn't giving up on herself. While she loved acting, doing the same parts over and over was killing her. Sometimes, she felt as if her life still hadn't begun. She was going to do whatever it took to set up her own audition. With or without Theo.

"I've got a few interviews lined up for you at your movie premiere next month," he said. "Is he going with you?"

He meaning Roberto. "He said he would."

"Good. Excellent," Theo said. "Oh, and one more thing."

"Yeah?"

"This upcoming cameo calls for him to kiss you. You okay with that?"

"I'm an actress, Theo. It's my job."

"Great, but let's make sure we leave the *sizzle* on the set, okay?"

Sizzle. That was the exact word the director had used when discussing this upcoming scene. He'd agreed that it was time for Mallory's *Racing Hearts* character to grow up a bit and must've talked with Theo and explained that no simple peck on the lips was going to do. It was about time.

She hung up the phone and a shot of adrenaline threw her stomach into a virtual somersault. Her director wanted Roberto to push it, push Mallory's character out of her comfort zone. And for Mallory to respond. For them to burn up the set with chemistry. *Sizzle*. This kiss was supposed to propel Mallory's character out of her bad engagement.

Two days ago, Mallory's director had taken her aside after taping and asked her if she thought Roberto "could manage heating up the set." Mallory had a feeling that heating things up wasn't going to be an issue. It was the cooling-off part that created the problem.

THE CONFERENCE ROOM was all but silent. Nathan Cargill had called a combined team meeting, including both sets of drivers, crew chiefs and car chiefs. Harry sat on Roberto's right side, Kent directly across the table, and Dean and Patsy Grosso on one end of the long table, opposite Nathan.

Nathan cleared his throat and gazed from one person to the next. "Today's meeting is long overdue, but I think it's about time we start working and thinking like one company."

It wasn't only this season's race record that seemed to be hurting. Cargill-Grosso Racing itself seemed to be falling apart at the seams. As if the Grossos' preoccupation with their investigation into baby Gina Grosso's kidnapping wasn't bad enough, nasty rumors had been circulating about Nathan since his dad had been murdered last December. Some homicide cop from the NYPD, a guy named Lucas Haines, had discovered that Nathan's business partner had been embezzling from their consulting business, insinuating that gave Nathan a financial motive for his dad's murder.

Roberto had heard all the rumors, but kept his nose out of it. As long as the situation didn't affect his ability to drive, people's personal lives were their own business.

"The success of this company all hinges on one thing." Nathan pointed first at Kent and then at Roberto. "You two getting along."

Kent wouldn't make eye contact with Roberto, and Roberto couldn't blame him. Not after what had happened in Bristol.

"The Atlanta races were uneventful." Dean Grosso tapped his pencil against the conference room tabletop. Roberto had finished fifteenth in the NASCAR Nationwide Series race on Saturday and eighteenth on Sunday in the NASCAR Sprint Cup Series race. Kent had done better. "But what the hell happened in Bristol?"

"Short track," Kent said. "Turns are too tight for Mr. Open-Wheel."

Roberto hated to admit it, but there was some truth to that statement. Short tracks, given they were under one mile in length, were definitely not Roberto's forte. In open-wheel, hitting another car was an almost sure ticket to a crash. But in stock car racing on a short track, it was either hit or be hit. Barrel on through, or get left behind. Bristol had proved that Roberto still had a lot to learn about driving stock cars.

Adrenaline had been high in Bristol, and no one's temper had been shorter than Roberto's. Midway through the race, he'd been pushed into Kent, costing his teammate a fender and, most likely, a couple of spots. Roberto had finished twenty-fifth, not good enough by his standards.

The only good part about Atlanta and Bristol was having Mallory there, sitting on the war wagon with Harry. And after the problems he'd had on Bristol's short track, he'd wanted to walk into her arms, wanted her to hold him, reassure him that he'd figure this whole NASCAR deal out. And she would've. She was that good a woman. Too good for him.

A soft tap sounded on the conference room door, interrupting their meeting. "I'm sorry." The Grossos' personal assistant stepped into the room and whispered to Dean and Patsy. They glanced at each other, and the pained expression on Patsy's face caused Roberto to look away for a moment. This had to be about their missing daughter.

"What's up?" Kent asked.

"An FBI agent's on the phone for us," Patsy explained.

"We'll take it in my office," Dean said, standing and heading toward the door.

Kent followed them and a few tense moments later, the three Grossos returned. While Dean and Patsy took their respective seats, Kent, clearly upset by whatever information had been relayed, walked to the window, keeping his back to the room.

"You all might as well hear it from us, rather than through the gossip channels," Patsy said. "The FBI is reopening the case concerning our daughter Gina's disappearance."

"So the information posted on that blog last month had merit?" Nathan asked.

Dean nodded. "But there's no way to determine who was responsible. Apparently, there are several ways to blog anonymously. Whoever posted that information knew what he or she was doing." Dean glanced at Patsy. "You'd better call Jake."

A few months ago, they'd hired Patsy's cousin and private investigator Jake McMasters to look into things outside of the FBI investigation.

"Last time I talked to him," Patsy said, "he was onto something. Maybe he'll be able to shed more light on the FBI's call."

Dean glanced around the room. "We'll get through this, folks. In the meantime, let's do what we can to work as a team. Okay?"

"We're all here for you two," Nathan said.

"We appreciate that, Nathan," Patsy said.

"All right then, where were we?" Dean said.

"Martinsville. This weekend," Nathan said.

Another short track. And Mallory wasn't able to make it due to a tight taping schedule for her show. After Martinsville, though, he had three speedway races in the next four weeks with a charity event scheduled in Mexico City on the open weekend. Roberto felt more at home with the high speeds and, although he'd still be driving his stock car at the Mexico City track, he couldn't wait to get back on the road course.

But with Martinsville looming on the horizon, Roberto had to accept the fact that he needed help. From his team. He shook his head at the realization that he couldn't do this on his own. Roberto was going to have to sit down and have a long chat with Harry and the rest of his team.

"You boys need a plan," Patsy said.

Kent turned around and glared at Roberto.

"We'll figure it out," Roberto said.

"You'd better," Kent said. "Because with teammates like you, we don't need enemies."

MALLORY SAT on the edge of the couch in her apartment watching the Martinsville race on TV. With only twenty laps to go, Roberto and Kent were poised to finish in the top five, and Roberto had run an excellent race. And it was a short track. She couldn't believe it.

"The No. 414 car has been running right behind the No. 507 car most of the day," an announcer said.

"He sure has," Payton Reese, lead sportscaster of the NSN program, agreed. *"Maybe Roberto Castillo has finally worked out his issues with teammate Kent Grosso."*

"I won't be holding my breath on that, but they're clearly making some progress."

"Only fifteen to go, and looks like they might both be finishing in the Top Ten— Oh, there goes Roberto Castillo, making his move on Zach Matheson."

"Go, go, go!" Mallory set her soda down on the table and clasped her hands together.

"He's pushing through on the inside."

"And Kent Grosso's right on Roberto's tail."

"Cargill-Grosso Racing could have two top-five finishes today."

"Yes!"

"If they pass Trey Sanford—"

"There they go!"

"Yes!" She jumped up and clapped.

"Hold on! Oh, no!"

"Did you see that?"

Roberto clipped Sanford's car. It'd happened so fast, Mallory didn't know for sure what'd happened.

"There goes Castillo. Into the wall!"

Mallory watched, a sick feeling in her stomach as Roberto's red-and-white No. 507 car veered toward the right and slammed into the wall. He spun, hitting Kent's rear fender and taking out two other cars.

"Well, that's going to shake things up."

"Will Kent Grosso be able to finish the race? That's the question."

"They'll pull off his fender and he'll lose a couple places but he'll finish."

Mallory watched the No. 507 car limp back to the Molloy Cycles garage. Roberto's first DNF—did not finish—not an auspicious beginning to his NASCAR career.

"And that'll be the end of it."

"Justin Murphy wins."

"And after a late-race crash, Kent Grosso comes in twentieth."

Aching for Roberto, Mallory watched the postrace interviews. Kent Grosso looked about ready to punch someone's lights out and Roberto gave short and clipped responses to reporters. She waited fifteen minutes, grabbed the phone and dialed his cell number. No answer.

ROBERTO COULDN'T REMEMBER the last time he'd been this mad. A DNF. *Dammit!* And he'd been so close to finishing in the top five. On a short track. He threw his gloves onto the garage floor and paced back and forth. Team members went about their business loading his smashed-up car into the hauler, but Roberto couldn't seem to clear his head.

"Dean and Nathan want to talk to everyone," Harry said. "So hang on." He pointed first at Roberto and then at Kent. "And you, too."

Roberto paced. Kent fumed.

A few minutes later, Nathan, Dean and Patsy showed up at the garage. "Our teams need some bonding time," Nathan said.

"We've got a van over at the front gate," Dean added. "Everyone climb in. We're all going for drinks and dinner."

So instead of being able to hightail it out of there and head home after the long race weekend, like they usually did, everyone was stuck. There were several groans and long faces. Roberto apparently wasn't the only one not interested in bonding time.

"You'll all get home in time to sleep in your own beds tonight," Nathan said. "After we do this."

Half an hour later, they were all seated in the privacy of a back room at a local bar and restaurant, hors d'oeuvres on the table and pitchers of beer flowing fast. Roberto sat back, sipped on a cola and listened to the conversation. The only other person at the table who hadn't loosened up and started enjoying himself was Kent.

He glared at Roberto across the table and Roberto couldn't help but glare right back. Whether the Grossos wanted it or not, he wasn't ready to bond. Not with Kent. Not yet. Maybe not ever.

While the other men at the table talked, drank, told jokes and generally had a good time, Nathan came to sit beside Roberto. "Have you given any consideration to staying in a motor home at the track?"

"Yes."

"And?"

"I prefer hotels."

Kent leaned forward across the table. "Let him stay in his damned penthouse suites, Nathan. No one wants him at the track any more than necessary."

Roberto glared at Kent, shoved himself away from the table and walked away. For the first time in a very long while he thought about grabbing a shot of tequila at the bar, or at least a beer, but that would set off a chain of events he'd regret in the morning. He headed for the bathroom to wash his face and cool off. When he came out of the restroom, the silhouette of a woman standing in the long, narrow hall blocked his path.

Son of a bitch. Just when he thought this night couldn't get any worse. "Hello, Kacy."

"Roberto."

He stayed where he was, keeping several feet between them. "I'm going to step out on a limb here and guess that you being in Martinsville, Virginia, isn't a coincidence."

"Hardly. Someone on your team at the track told me where I could find you."

"Wonderful." She was backlit by lights and he couldn't see her face, but he was sure she was up to no good. "So where do you have the photographer hiding tonight?" He glanced past her toward the bar. From what he could tell, there was no one who didn't belong here.

"There's no photographer. Just you and me."

"What do you want, Kacy?"

She stepped right up to him, blocking his exit, and ran a hand down his chest. "For you to notice me." The smell of alcohol came off her in waves. "Would it be so hard for you to give me a few crumbs of attention?"

"I'm afraid that would be leading you on." He narrowed his eyes at her, not trusting her or her motive for one second. "And I'm not the least bit interested."

"Come on, Roberto. Loosen up. We had fun." She pressed her lips together in a pretty pout. "The casinos. The clubs. Dancing. Remember the mambo?"

Somehow, he'd found himself on a dance floor with her. She'd certainly known her moves, that was for sure. "You are drunk, Kacy. But you need to accept there's never going to be anything between us."

"I miss you." She moved even closer. "We had a chance at something special." She reached out, slid open a button on his shirt, slipped her hand under his shirt.

"There was no *we*." Although he grabbed her wrist and stopped her progress, her fingertips continued to explore his chest. He felt his nipple harden at the contact, an instinctive response, no more. And he breathed a sigh of relief.

Not all that long ago, he would've been all over this action. Back then, his attitude would've been why the hell not? Tonight, he couldn't stop asking himself why? *Because he could* didn't seem to be much of a reason any longer.

That wasn't all there was to it, though. Thoughts of Mallory kept popping into his head. He didn't want to hurt her, and if this made it into the papers that's what would happen. Times like this he hated his public life.

He looked down at Kacy, with her hand all over his chest, and he felt nothing but distaste. The realization made him smile.

"My God!" she whispered. "Mallory Dalton has you whipped."

The fact that this statement might actually be true didn't bother him in the slightest. He only hated that Kacy knew. He wished he could keep Mallory all to himself, keep the world out of their lives, shelter them from the Kacys of this world. "Move on, Kacy. There are a lot greener pastures out there."

As if a challenge had been issued, Kacy advanced, backing him against the wall. He put his hands out to his sides and refused to touch her. "You need help, Kacy. Some kind of treatment program. I can call your dad, if you want."

She glared at him. "Keep my dad out of this." She reached for his belt buckle and he stopped her hand. "I'll bet you haven't even slept with her yet, have you?" She hooked a hand around his neck.

And Roberto saw a flash of light. He jerked his head toward the bar area, but there were no photographers. No one suspicious. Only patrons lined up at the bar. It must have been his imagination.

"I'll bet she won't do it." Kacy kept going. "I'll bet America's Sweetheart is as pure as the virgin snow."

He shifted out of her reach.

"No one's watching. No one needs to know."

"I'd know." He set her back away from him. "Time to go, Kacy. I have nothing for you. Not now. Not ever. Except for getting you some help with your problems."

"You're sure about that?"

"Positive."

She dragged a fingernail across his cheek. "A tiger can hide in the brush for a long while, Roberto, camouflaging his stripes." Then she puckered her lips and blew him a kiss. "But eventually he'll have to come out to satisfy his hunger."

CHAPTER EIGHT

MALLORY SAT IN HER dressing room at the Charlotte studio and stared at the pictures in the newspaper. Earlier that morning, one of the other *Racing Hearts* cast members had been quick to shove the entertainment section of the morning paper in Mallory's face. With her eyebrows raised and a grin on her face, the woman had said, "You're in way over your head. *Sweetheart.*"

Considering the less-than-supportive source, Mallory had folded the paper and stashed it away for later. First and foremost, she had scenes to act out and a job to do. Whatever bad news was in the paper, and she was sure it had to be bad, could wait. She'd put it off until lunchtime, when she'd known she could count on some privacy, and had flipped the paper open.

Roberto with Kacy Haughton. In a narrow hallway. Her hand was around his neck and her face tilted toward him as if the photographer had narrowly missed a kiss. The intent on Kacy's face was clear. She'd set her sights on Roberto, and, based on body posture in the pictures, she'd succeeded. The two looked intimate and involved.

Why she was so surprised was beyond her. She should've known this was going to happen. But then maybe surprise wasn't precisely what she was feeling. Blindsided maybe, especially when she looked at the photo of herself the paper had chosen to display next to those of Roberto and Kacy. She had sunglasses on and was looking down, a slight frown on her face.

The crazy thing was that Mallory had lost those particular sunglasses ages ago. That photo of her had to be months old. By their choice of photos, the paper had managed to make it look as if this was her reaction to Roberto and Kacy. They'd manipulated the situation to tell their own story. In entertainment news, the truth didn't matter. All that mattered was selling papers.

Even the heading over the photos was ridiculous: On Again? Off Again? Then the caption pointed out that Mallory had been noticeably absent from the Martinsville race, as if there had been a connection between her absence and Kacy's appearance.

Unable to resist, she looked again at Roberto's profile next to Kacy's. Maybe blindsided didn't quite hit the nail on the head for what Mallory was feeling. *Jealousy.* That was probably more like it. Silly, really, given she had no claims on Roberto. She had no right to that emotion. No right to be angry. No right to be hurt. But she was all of those things. Because she'd started to care about him. Roberto had been right. It was clearly only a matter of time before he broke her heart and tossed it out for the media to feast upon.

A knock sounded on her dressing room door. "They're ready for your next scene, Mallory."

"Is he here yet?"

"Who?"

"Roberto Castillo."

"He's in the building and on his way up."

Her heart raced and she started shaking. She had to kiss the man. For the first time. On the lips. In front of cast and crew.

"You're an actress," she whispered to herself. "You can do this." She took a deep breath and opened the door.

In way over her head? Hell, she was drowning.

USED TO BE the lies didn't bother him. Not anymore.

Roberto drove his sports car into the parking space reserved for him for this afternoon's taping at the Charlotte studio, turned off the purring engine and held perfectly still for a minute. A newspaper, crumpled and discarded, sat on the passenger seat. He'd had to buy one after Patricia had called to read him the riot act, but he should've saved himself the trouble.

At first, he couldn't figure out how someone had managed to get a picture of him and Kacy in that restroom hallway in Martinsville, and then he remembered the flash from the bar area. Kacy had left him a voice mail swearing she'd had nothing to do with the photo, but it didn't matter. The damage was done.

How was he supposed to act as if nothing had happened? Oh, hell. He never would've believed a day would come when he wouldn't be looking forward to a "sizzling hot kiss" and "some skin," as the director had called it. There was no doubt he wanted to kiss Mallory. Hell, he wanted to do a lot more than that, but doing it in front of a camera would seem bizarre. Kissing her with the Kacy mess hanging over his head would be worse.

Then again, what was the worst that could happen? Mallory could call off their *arrangement* and he could focus on his driving. Maybe that wouldn't be such a bad thing.

He left his car and headed into the building. A production person, assigned to hold his hand, took him to the stage where they were currently taping a different scene for the show. He glanced around, hoping to find Mallory and talk with her before taping began. She was neither on the set nor amongst the production crew.

"Very nice, people," the director called. "Let's move on. Stage six."

The entire crew moved to a different set and Roberto was directed to join them. Still Mallory was nowhere to be found. The director ran through the scene with him, and then yelled, "Where the hell is Mallory?"

"I'm here." She emerged from the darkness at the edge of the set. "Sorry." She wouldn't look at him. Obviously, she knew about the newest Kacy photo.

"Mallory," Roberto said. "Can we talk for a minute?"

"There's nothing to say." This time she did look at him, but her features held no discernible emotion.

"So you are ready for this?"

"Sure. Why not?" A slight edge to her voice was the only indication there was a problem.

Suddenly, he was angry. Angry that he had to explain. Sick and tired of always taking the blame. For everything. "If that's the way you want it," he said. "Let's get this over with."

The scene was to take place during an evening party sponsored by NASCAR. Mallory's character was the daughter of a famous racing figure and the scene began as she stepped outside, supposedly for some fresh air. Roberto took his position in the shadows and waited.

"Five, four, three, two, and…" The assistant director started the cameras rolling and Mallory walked through some French doors and onto a fake veranda with a drink in her hand.

Roberto held out for his cue.

Mallory closed her eyes and took a deep breath.

The assistant director signaled for Roberto to move, and he stepped onto the veranda. "Hot in there, isn't it?"

Mallory looked surprised. "I'm sorry. I didn't know anyone was out here." She stepped backward.

"Don't go." He touched her arm. Although he felt her stiffen, he doubted anyone else noticed. "I like your company."

"I'm engaged, Roberto."

"You shouldn't be. He's all wrong for you."

"How would you know?"

He glanced down at her lips, wishing they were alone, wishing she understood. "I'll show you." He took her drink from her, set it on the veranda rail and stepped toward her.

She stiffened and glared at him, not at all what she was supposed to do.

"Cut," the director called from his booth. "Again. From the beginning."

Every time Roberto touched her, Mallory tensed. They had to begin the scene over three times. After the last time, the director came onto the set and approached Mallory. "Sweetheart, what's going on?"

"It doesn't feel right." She swallowed. "He's supposed to kiss me, not me kiss him. Right?"

"Yes."

"I'm engaged. I'm not going to politely let him take me in his arms."

"All right. Let's try something different." The director turned to Roberto. "Can you get a little…forceful?"

"Sure." He glowered at Mallory. "If that's the way she wants it."

"Let's go again, people." He turned to Roberto. "Remember, you finally have Mallory alone. And you're not used to waiting for women. You've wanted this for a long, long time."

Then he turned toward Mallory, rubbed her arms. "A little bit of reluctance is okay. But remember, it's close to midnight. You've had a few drinks, and you're feeling nice and soft and loose. This is the scene that turns you. This kiss is so powerful that you call off your engagement. Right?"

"Right." Mallory took a deep breath, loosened her shoulders. Someone dropped a couple fake ice cubes into her glass with the intention of keeping the scene looking fresh.

"Ready?" the director asked.

"Ready," she said.

Roberto walked onto the veranda once again and went through his lines, feeling this time as if he wasn't acting at all. Every fiber in him was tuned in to Mallory. This time, he was determined to have her in his arms. This time, when he reached for her and she jerked away, he wasn't going to let go. This was going to be one first kiss she would never forget.

"This is why you shouldn't marry him," he declared and jerked her into his arms. Holding her tightly, despite her squirming and pushing against his chest, he kissed her, thoroughly and completely. There was no acting involved. He wanted her.

She stopped wriggling and went still. He urged her mouth open and when her tongue touched his, Roberto lost all track of the people on the set around him. He picked her up, set her on top of the rail and stepped between her legs.

The moment she began kissing him back, he forgot they were being taped, forgot they were supposed to be acting. All he knew was her taste, her soft lips beneath the pressure of his own, the way her hands explored his sides and finally settled at his back.

She whimpered, as lost in sensation as he was, and wrapped her legs around him. Time and place slipped away.

"Cut! That's a wrap."

At the fringe of his consciousness, Roberto heard the director's order, but didn't care. Apparently, neither did Mallory. Her tongue dipped and danced with his, and her breathing turned ragged.

"I said cut. Cut!"

Roberto pulled back and took a deep breath, regaining his equilibrium. He scooped her off the rail, set her on her feet, but her knees almost buckled, as if she hadn't the strength to stand. She looked the way he felt, completely dazed.

"Perfect!" the director called out from his booth. "You two have boiling chemistry. Love it. Love it. Love it!"

Mallory blinked, pushed his hands away and stalked off the set.

"*Espérate*. Mallory. Wait!" The bright lights shining in his face kept him from seeing where she was going. He shaded his eyes, stepped off the set. "Where's Mallory's dressing room?" he asked the assistant director.

"Down that hall and on the left." The man smiled and pointed behind him. "Nice moves."

Roberto strode in the direction the man had sent him, found a door marked with Mallory's name and knocked.

"Go away," she said.

He turned the knob. Locked. "We need to talk."

"There's nothing to say."

"I won't leave. You know it."

After a long moment of complete silence, she opened the door and stepped back. "Let's get this over with, then."

He went into the small room and closed the door behind him. "On second thought, I'm not sure talking will do us any good. Maybe instead we'd better pick up where we left off. Without the cameras." He drew her into his arms and pressed his mouth against hers. Only now, she hung like a limp rag in his arms. He set her away from him. "I know what I felt out there. You can't tell me you don't want this."

"I'm an actress. Remember?" She swatted a rolled newspaper at his chest and crossed her arms. "I really don't want *you.*"

He tossed the newspaper down onto the sofa.

"So you've seen it?" she asked.

He nodded.

"I want to know one thing. When were those photos taken?"

"Right after the Martinsville race." There had to have been a photographer behind the bar.

When he didn't provide any more details, she glared at him. "Well? Aren't you going to say anything else? Don't I deserve an explanation?"

He shrugged and glanced around her dressing room, an area only large enough for a couch, table, makeup chair and mirror. "There's nothing else to say."

"How can you be so arrogant that you don't feel the need to explain? Can you or can you not refute what's in these pictures?"

"What do you *see* in those pictures?"

"You and Kacy Haughton together, very close."

"Yep. That's about it. *No más. No menos.*"

"We had a deal," she said. "Our arrangement is supposed to be exclusive."

"It was and it is."

"Looks to me like you'd just kissed her."

Resolutely, he shook his head. "Now that, I can assure you, did not happen." He couldn't get Mallory's kiss out of his mind, the way her mouth had felt, warm and responsive. The way she'd looked up at him after he'd drawn away, her lips swollen, red and slightly parted.

"That's it? That's all you're going to say?"

He crossed his arms, clenched his jaw. He'd said enough, more than he'd planned. If it wasn't sufficient, too bad.

Mallory moved across the room, putting the coffee table between them. "You're right. I have no business asking you all these questions and expecting an explanation. I don't have a right to tell you not to see other women. If you want to sleep with every woman you meet, that's your prerogative."

Her reaction astounded and softened him.

She spun around. "But you agreed to maintain, at the very least, the *pretense* of an exclusive relationship with me."

"Yes, I did."

"So that's what I expect. No more. No less." She glanced out the window. "This happens again, whether it's true or not, our arrangement is over."

"Mallory," he whispered.

She wouldn't look at him.

He didn't want to have to explain. He wasn't sure what he expected of her in this situation, but for once he wanted a woman to believe in him. In *him*. Regardless of what he said, or didn't say. What the press published, or didn't publish. Unfortunately, that wasn't going to happen. Not here. Not now. Probably not ever.

He should say something more. He didn't want to hurt her, felt bad that he'd caused her pain. An explanation, an excuse was at the tip of his tongue, hanging there, waiting to be voiced. "I'll figure out a way to make this ri—"

"Take me with you to Mexico City," she said.

He stared at her.

"For that charity event you're racing."

"Why? What will that solve?"

"It's as close to a home turf as you're going to get for a while, right?"

"Yes," he said tentatively, trying to figure this out. He'd driven that track too many times to count.

"You probably have a huge fan base there, watching every move you make, right?"

"Yeah."

"Well, the way I see it, taking me with you to Mexico makes the situation perfectly clear. To everyone. *That* will set everything right."

"In other words, it tells the world that Kacy Haughton means nothing to me." And that Mallory Dalton was special. He was beginning to worry this might be true.

"Something like that."

Smart move. Still, there was something about it that didn't feel right. "Was this your agent's idea?"

"No." She looked away.

No, Theo Stein would not have wanted this. Interesting. "Okay," he said, against his—lately—better judgment. "You will come to Mexico with me."

CHAPTER NINE

MALLORY FLIPPED excitedly through the Mexico City guidebook she'd purchased after wrapping up taping for the day at the Charlotte track. She sat on the old sofa in the living room of Tara's apartment, absorbing the unfamiliar Spanish names of the city's districts, restaurants and sites of interest. Though she'd only been able to finagle a few days off the *Racing Hearts* schedule, she couldn't wait for her first trip to a foreign land.

The fact that she'd coerced Roberto into taking her was beside the point. This world-traveler kind of publicity was exactly what she needed to help broaden her image. Her old TV character, sweet little Amy Mitchell, never would've flown out of the country, but it was about time that all-grown-up-and-ready-to-experience-life Mallory Dalton got her passport stamped.

She tried very hard not to think about how this trip could potentially reflect badly on Roberto for *corrupting* America's Sweetheart. He was a big boy. He could handle it.

A loud knock sounded on Tara's apartment door. Although Mallory stayed at her sister's apartment whenever she was taping in Charlotte, she still felt like a guest. That meant the door was not hers to answer.

"See who's there, would ya?" Tara yelled from her bedroom.

Mallory set the guidebook down on the coffee table and hopped up to look through the peephole. Two men stood in the hall. "Who is it?"

"Delivery for Mallory Dalton."

"What?" She looked again and noticed the name of an elite

department store listed on the packages they had stacked on two dollies. This was odd. She opened the door.

"Who's here?" Her shoulder-length blond hair swinging, Tara appeared.

"A delivery. For me."

"Cool!" Tara grinned, and her bright blue eyes flashed with excitement.

"Where do you want 'em?" the older man asked, still standing in the hall.

"What is all this?" she asked.

He handed her an envelope, and she tore it open to find a small card scribbled with the words, *Try some new colors. New styles. For Mexico.*

Her sister snatched the note out of Mallory's hand. "Who's it from?"

"Roberto." Mallory hesitated.

"Well, for heaven's sake." Tara yanked Mallory back out of the doorway. "Set them over there." She pointed toward the living room.

They pushed the dollies into the apartment and stacked the boxes, four to five high, all along one wall. There had to be at least thirty. "We need you to sign for these," the guy apparently in charge said, flipping through his paperwork.

Mallory hesitated, unsure what to do. The last time she'd seen Roberto, she'd been mad enough to take his head clear off, and she still wasn't sure if her anger had been honestly related exclusively to the Kacy picture, or if a part of her reaction had to do with his kiss on the set. Or, more accurately, how she'd kissed him back. Even a day later, the memory of it came close to making her swoon.

"Can you wait a minute?" she asked the men.

"Sure."

"Well." Tara laughed, clearly excited. "Open them."

The first box held a daytime dress in a wild print of royal-blue, green and black, black sandals, heavy gold jewelry and a funky black purse, all sporting designer labels. A flirty black evening dress splattered with red, lime-green, orange and purple exotic flowers was in the next box, along with chunky bangles in matching colors and strappy black sandals.

"Oh my God," Tara whispered. "Those outfits will look gorgeous on you."

"They're too bold."

"Bold is perfect on you. If you don't believe me, go look."

Mallory did believe her sister, but she went to the mirror in Tara's bedroom anyway and held each dress to her chin. The dazzling colors highlighted the golden tones in her skin and worked in perfect counterpoint to her dark hair and eyes. She flashed on how she'd looked in the red dress Roberto had bought for her in Vegas, remembered how she'd felt more and more comfortable wearing it as the night had worn on. Maybe she should be stepping out of that clothing comfort zone on her own.

"Incredible," her sister said from the doorway. "Those dresses look like they were made with you in mind."

"Hey!" one of the delivery guys yelled from back at the apartment door. "Can we go now?"

"Yeah, go ahead." Tara ran into the living room, signed their forms and closed the door behind them.

Mallory went back out to the living room and opened the next box and the next, not stopping until she and Tara had checked out the majority of the contents. Part of her felt giddy, like a kid on Christmas morning. The other part of her couldn't help but feel as if she were being bought in some way.

He'd sent her everything from blouses to suits to formal dresses. The fabrics were mouthwatering, the styles form-fitting, confident and trendy, unlike anything she would've picked out for herself. All of the colors were bold: orange, black, white, gold, turquoise and, of course, red. There wasn't a subtle pastel in the lot. Every outfit came fully accessorized with shoes, purses, sunglasses and jewelry. He'd even thought to include swimsuits—bikinis, of course—and track attire, several outfits in the No. 507 team colors of red and white.

"Is all this going to fit?" Tara asked.

Mallory glanced at the labels. She couldn't believe it. "How did he know my size?"

"He's a man who loves women. I'm guessing he's done this before."

Tara had to be right, and Mallory cringed. This was so like him to try and put a woman in her place.

"I'll say one thing," Tara said. "He sure knows what'll look good on you. I've been trying for years to get you to buy these colors. Why don't you ever wear them?"

Old feelings of not fitting in surfaced, and Mallory took a deep breath. She swallowed as a painful memory surfaced. "You probably don't remember this, but Mom bought me a red dress when I was thirteen. She said it was my color. I was excited to wear it for Christmas that year, but when the pictures came back all I noticed was how different I looked from the rest of you."

"You're not different, Mal. You've got Great-Grandma Clara's coloring. That's all. And you're lucky for it, if you ask me."

Their father's grandmother had been Greek and the only one in the entire Dalton relation with dark hair. "No, Tara. I am different." Mallory glanced around and reached for the family photo her sister had framed and placed on a side table. "Look at the picture. I stand out like a thorn among roses."

Tara took the picture and studied it. "How 'bout a rose amidst a bunch of blue-eyed daisies."

"That's my point. I remember looking at all our family pictures and wondering, why me?" She'd always felt as if she were on the outside looking in, wanting to be a part of something and never quite making the grade.

"But, Mallory, you're beautiful."

Mallory stood and paced. "I want to fit in somewhere, Tara, anywhere. That's all I've ever wanted. To fit in." She glanced around at all the packages, the rainbow of colors. It was every woman's dream—an entirely new wardrobe in one fell swoop. And it was too much. "I can't keep any of this stuff."

"What?" Tara's mouth dropped open.

"It's not right." She opened the sliding door to Tara's balcony, stepped outside and was happy to find the delivery truck still in the parking lot. "Hey!" she yelled.

One of the men looked out through his open window. Clearly, they were about to drive away.

"Come back. Please! All of these packages have to go back to the store."

"You serious?" he yelled.

"As a heart attack!" She slid the door closed again and turned around.

Tara, shaking her head at her, held out a large box. "You forgot one."

Mallory opened it and a shiny teal color winked at her from beneath several folds of tissue paper.

"What is it?"

"I don't know." She whisked her fingertips across the silky-soft fabric and found a note. *Your movie premiere deserves something special, Roberto.* One of the most important events of her life was coming up in two days, and she still hadn't found anything to wear. The director of *Three Sisters* would be there and she had no clue what would impress him.

Tara read over her shoulder. "Well…" she urged. "Let's see."

Mallory flipped back the paper. "It's a dress." Made by an atrociously expensive designer. She had to admit, she always drooled over the designer labels whenever she went shopping, but her acting salary still hadn't reached the levels to put this particular designer within her budget.

She held up the dress. The fabric was heavy and stretchy, meant to cling to every curve. The shoulder straps were wide, the neckline low and revealing. The bodice was tight fitting and gathered at the front and center, from chest to belly button. There was a coordinating jacket with wide lapels and flashy silver buttons.

"If you don't keep that," Tara said, shaking her head, "you're insane."

In the same box, he'd also included a wide rhinestone wrist cuff, a set of dangling silver earrings, a small silver clutch and the prettiest pair of shoes Mallory had ever held in her hands.

They were silver-colored pumps with tall, narrow heels and made by another ultrafamous designer. This ensemble probably cost close to a year's rent on Mallory's apartment.

She laid the dress back down in the box and closed the cover. "I guess you'd better call the funny farm and have me committed."

"Mallory." Tara followed her around the apartment. "This is a small dent in the man's bank account. I'm going to guess he won't notice."

"He's not my husband, fiancé or boyfriend," Mallory said resolutely. "And I refuse to be put in my place."

ROBERTO GLANCED one more time at the address the *Racing Hearts* people had given him and slammed on the brakes outside Tara Dalton's apartment building. Mallory had wanted to go to Mexico City and he wanted her to go in style.

But dammit! He was running late, and he'd wanted to be here before the delivery. He'd wanted to see Mallory's face when she opened all the packages. Disappointed, he climbed out of his sports car and walked slowly toward the front door, pocketing his keys.

"Yeah, I know!" he heard a man yelling from the side parking lot. "We're running late. We're heading toward the next address right now."

Roberto glanced around the building and saw the front end of what looked like a big truck. He followed the voices and found two men standing at the back end of a delivery truck with dollies loaded down with packages. Given the store name printed on the side of the boxes, they were most likely Mallory's. One of the men was on his cell phone.

It looked as if they hadn't yet been to her apartment. Roberto was in luck. "Wait a minute!" he yelled. "I need to talk to Mallory Dalton before you deliver those packages."

"You're too late," said the older man, the one with the phone.

"We already took everything up," the younger one explained. "And now we're returning it to the store."

He glanced back and forth between them. "What are you talking about?"

"She wouldn't accept it. Wanted us to take it all back."

"Chicks." The younger man shook his head. "Go figure."

Increíble. Roberto had wanted to do something nice for Mallory. And she'd rejected it. Honestly, it felt as if she'd rejected him. He didn't know why he'd expected anything different from a woman. His gut churned and his first reaction was to leave. If that was the way she wanted it, fine. But as his initial surge of anger subsided, hurt settled. Old insecurities surfaced. He flashed on his mother slamming the door in his face. The ultimate in rejection for a young boy.

No. This wasn't over.

"Don't return anything," he said. "Have the store ship every single box to Manhattan and bill me for the shipping. I'll call you with an address."

"You sure?"

"Positive." He slipped them two hundred-dollar bills.

"Okay," the older driver said. "You got it."

"Thank you." Roberto climbed the steps to Tara's floor and knocked at the appropriate apartment.

Several seconds later, Mallory appeared, opening the door with a jerk. "You shouldn't have done that." She glared at him.

Dios, she was even gorgeous when she was angry. "Can I come in?"

"Why should I care?" Mallory turned away.

He remained in the hall, debating.

A pretty blonde, several inches taller than Mallory, appeared from the depths of the apartment. "Hi, I'm Tara." She quickly shook his hand and actually seemed rather worried for him. "Mallory's sister."

"Hi."

"Exit, stage left." She snatched up her purse and came through the door as if a fire nipped at her heels. When she saw the delivery truck outside, she whispered, "You're not seriously going to return all that, are you?"

"They're shipping it to Manhattan."

Tara raised her eyebrows at Roberto and mouthed, "Good luck."

Roberto, still upset, confused and more unsure of himself than he'd been in a long, long while, stepped into the apartment and closed the door behind him. He found Mallory in the kitchen taking a soda out of the refrigerator. "Mallory." When she wouldn't look at him, he tried to explain. "I meant to be here before the delivery, but I got held up in a meeting at Cargill-Grosso headquarters."

"It wouldn't have made a difference. I still would've sent everything back."

"I would have had the chance to explain before you jumped to any…a…a…" he said, tapping his forehead, unable to think of the word. "Conclusions. *Erróneo.*"

"Erroneous? Then explain to me why you bought all that stuff." She turned and studied him. "That's all I want to know. Why?"

"Porque puedo," he said, lapsing into Spanish. "Because I can. It's pretty much as simple as that. Why did you send it all back?"

"Because I… It doesn't… I can't…" She spun away from him, clearly frustrated. "The clothes aren't me."

"How do you know unless you try them on, wear them, live in them?"

"All those bright colors and clingy fabrics. They're not my style."

"I understand. You want to fit in, belong. But your beauty, your body shouldn't be hidden. Simply to fit in."

She paced back and forth in the small kitchen and then turned on him, angry. And hurt, too, like him. "You…you only want a trophy on your arm," she said. "That's all."

Ah. He saw this situation from her side. She felt belittled. "Is it so wrong to want you to look your most beautiful? Wouldn't it be worse to hide you away? Keep you to myself?"

"So you want me to look all decked out? Like Kacy Haughton?"

"No!" he yelled. "I don't want you to look anything like Kacy."

She turned her back on him.

He stepped toward her, gently touched her shoulders and turned her around. "I have so much, Mallory. More than I ever dreamed. I wanted to do something for you. Humor me."

"It feels like you're buying me. With clothes."

"No! Dammit! You are reading something into it that's not there." Oh, hell, he couldn't win this. No way. No how. But he had to try. "Mallory, you are twisting things around."

"We have a business deal. This is not personal."

Screw it!

"Pues, si quiero hacerlo personal? Si quiero más?" He wrapped his fingers around her neck, rubbed his thumb over her lips. "What if I want to make it personal? What if I want more?"

She blinked. Her head fell back, heavy in his hand, and he wrapped his other arm around her waist. With her head tilted, her lips were right there, in front of him, a breath away. That's when he realized they weren't merely words thrown out in the heat of a fight. He really did want more. No more agents arranging their schedules. No more publicity photos. No more pretending. No more kisses staged for a camera.

He wanted them to be real. He bent and kissed her, holding her tight against him. She stiffened, hesitating, before her resistance completely failed. She kissed him back, melted against him.

"I want you," he whispered. "All of you. *Basta de juegos.* No more games." Kissing her lips, her cheeks, her neck, he backed her out of the kitchen and down the hall, into the bedroom. It was probably Tara's but, in the heat of this moment, he would've taken her anywhere. He drew her back with him onto the sleigh bed and rolled, leaning over her and brushing her long hair away from her face. "I have wanted this for weeks."

She stiffened under him. "So you buy me clothes." She put her hands on his chest and pushed him away. "You're arrogant. Full of yourself. And I don't want your…your…payment." She jumped up. "I can't help but shake the feeling that this is your way of reminding me I am just one of many women who have passed through your life. Dress me up. Take me out. I'm nothing more than an accessory to you."

No. That wasn't true.

"You do this all the time, don't you? With women. Buy them things. Clothes. Jewelry. Maybe even art or furniture."

He wanted to argue, tell her she was the first woman he had ever bought anything for, but he couldn't. So what?

Clenching his jaw tight, he stood. "Arrogant and full of myself. Yes. On those counts you are right. I'm also opinionated, stubborn and competitive. But I have never, ever *bought* a woman in my life. Believe it or not, I have not needed to. I have been enough, all on my own."

He stalked toward the door and turned. "Everything's being shipped to your apartment in Chelsea," he yelled. "Throw all the clothes in a Dumpster for all I care."

CHAPTER TEN

"Is HE THERE yet?" Tara asked.

"No," Mallory said into her cell phone. "But I think he'll be here."

She stood in the foyer of her apartment building waiting for the limo to pick her up for the movie premiere. The big question of the evening was whether or not Roberto would be accompanying her. They hadn't spoken directly to each other since their fight at Tara's apartment two days ago, and, if she was honest with herself, she missed the sound of his voice.

No, that wasn't true. She missed *him*. And she hadn't been able to get him, or his kisses, both from the *Racing Hearts* set and Tara's apartment, out of her mind.

Though she'd been extremely busy taping, due to a few rewrites on her character, she'd had a lot of time to think, and she always came back to one indisputable fact—this was Roberto Castillo. *The* Roberto Castillo. The playboy, the bad boy, the man who would never be tied down to one woman. She'd have to be insane to think she could change that. It would be best for everyone to put this relationship back on the straight and narrow. This was a business arrangement designed to further two careers. No more, no less.

Still, she hadn't been able to resist sending him a dress shirt to wear for tonight's premiere. She'd seen it in a window on Fifth Avenue and immediately imagined him in it. An Armani in a burgundy-and-black swirl print, the shirt was one of the more expensive individual pieces of clothing she'd ever purchased. With any luck, he'd give her the chance to even the score.

Although she'd had the shirt delivered to Roberto's apartment and sent him several messages via their agents, Theo hadn't, as of six o'clock tonight, returned her latest call. The plan had been for the limo to pick Roberto up at his condo in the Upper West Side, stop at her place in Chelsea and then continue on to the reception before the premiere showing of the movie in East Greenwich Village.

"Dammit," Tara muttered. "I should've caught a flight. This is too important an event for you to go alone."

"He'll be here."

"You have a lot more faith in the man than I do."

Call her naive—who didn't?—but Mallory had chosen to think the best of Roberto. He knew how important this was to her, and she refused to believe he was cruel.

"When is the car supposed to be there?" Tara asked.

Mallory glanced at her watch. "Five minutes ago."

Feeling a bit claustrophobic in the foyer, she stepped out onto the sidewalk. For an April evening, the air was chillier than normal, and she wrapped her jacket a little tighter around herself. Then she saw the limo coming down the street. "The car's here."

"Did he come?"

She could see the driver and waved, but with the darkened windows there was no way to tell if Roberto was already in the back. "I don't know."

The limo double-parked in front of her building and the driver hopped out at the same time as the back door opened. Roberto stepped out onto the street. "He did come," she whispered. "I gotta go!" She slipped the phone into her purse.

Roberto's gaze caught hers and then traveled the whole length of her, head to toe. Clenching his jaw, he looked away for a moment, as if to gather his emotions, but when he glanced back, the look in his eye was anything but anger. He stepped between two parked cars and onto the sidewalk. "My imagination didn't come close to this reality."

In that instant all her posturing to keep her distance, all her plans to treat him like a business associate flew right out the window. "I'm sorr—"

"Shh." He put a finger to her lips.

"I need to say this." She smoothed down the fabric of the teal dress he'd bought specifically for her for this night. "You did something very nice for me and I was…out of line."

"No," he whispered. "You were right. I'll never buy you anything again."

She grinned. "Can we have fun tonight?"

"It's your night, *querida*. We can do whatever you want." He held his hand toward her.

She reached out and squeezed his fingers. "Thank you for coming."

"I'm not sure a race would have kept me away." Wearing a black suit and the shirt she'd sent to him without a tie, he looked sexy hip, and infinitely comfortable in his own skin.

"You don't look so bad yourself." She gave a little tug on his lapel. "Nice shirt, huh?"

He wouldn't take his eyes off her. "At least someone knows what I like."

A short while later, the limo approached the Cinema Village. Mallory glanced out the darkened window, waiting for their turn to drive up to the red carpet area sectioned off at the front of the theater. Fans, lined up along the road, craned their necks, peering this way and that, hoping—dying, really—for a glimpse into the backseat. No one could see her, but still, she already felt on display.

Two or three vehicles ahead of them, the headlining star of the movie, a well-established young actor, got out of his limo and reached back for the hand of his well-established actress wife. Mallory's stomach took a nosedive when she saw the man had dressed in a classic black tux and his wife in a stunning, full-length strapless gown of pale green silk with a full, fluffy skirt. They stood confidently in the center of the red carpet, turning first one way and then the other, smiling for photographers, chatting comfortably with the director and producers and looking like royalty.

Next was the headlining actress. Her rock-star husband, dressed in a shimmering gray suit and white dress shirt, jumped out of the backseat and waved before holding out a hand for his wife. She was gorgeous in a red silk dress with a plunging neckline and a flowing train. They both looked so comfortable and poised, having no doubt done this kind of thing many times.

This was Mallory's first premiere. What if she tripped? These heels were so high she could easily stumble and fall flat on her face. What if the critics hated her dress, her hair, the purse, the shoes? Maybe she should be wearing sandals instead of pumps? Maybe the jacket was too much? She could end up on the cover of any number of magazines voted worst dressed actress on the planet. What if—

"Hey." Roberto laid his hand over hers. "You'll do fine."

How did he know?

"You are stunning and you can hold your own next to anyone out there. And besides—" he raised his brows "—you've got me."

She grinned, already feeling better. "*The* Roberto Castillo."

"No. That's not what I meant." He brought the back of her hand to his mouth and planted a kiss. "I'll get out first and hold my hand out for you. I won't let you fall or trip. I have your back. Okay?"

The telltale sign of emotion tingled in her throat and her eyes welled with tears.

"Oh, no. None of that." He gave a quick shake to his head. "Think about something else. Think about..." He ran his hand along the inside of her calf, went further to graze the inside of her knee.

When it seemed as if he might reach higher still, she quickly clenched her thighs together, trapping his hand. "*What* are you doing?"

"It's working, isn't it? Getting you to think about something else." He grinned. "Like how it feels to have my mouth on your lips."

All thoughts of the crowd outside flew from her mind as she looked into his eyes.

"I've kissed a lot of women. But none of them have felt like you." His fingers inched farther up her legs. "Later," he whispered. "When we are alone. I'm going to take that gorgeous dress off you. Inch by inch." He closed his eyes. "I'm imagining it now. You. Naked. So beautiful."

"Stop it."

"Come back to my place." He opened his eyes. They seemed darker, more intense than normal. "Spend the night with me, Mallory."

"No."

"You want it as much as I do."

"Yes," she whispered.

"What's stopping you?" At the moment she couldn't remember. Good thing the limo door opened. She let go of the breath she'd been holding and pushed him toward the sidewalk. "So go already!"

He climbed outside, turned and held out his hand. His grip felt strong and sure, and her fears and insecurities dissipated, like air being let out of a balloon. "Thank you," she whispered, looking into his eyes.

"De nada." He smiled at her, a gesture so full of compassion, understanding and support that she, miraculously, relaxed even more. "But I meant every word."

Straightening her shoulders, she stepped outside into the fading sunlight. He wrapped her hand around the hard muscles of his arm and remained still for a moment while she gained her footing. He held her hand across the red carpet, stopped for the requisite photos and stayed by her side during the entire pre-premiere reception.

"Wasn't there someone here you wanted to meet?" he asked.

She glanced at the crowd. "A director. He's scheduled to do a movie a friend of mine wrote."

"That's the sister part you wanted?"

"Mmm-hmm. He's over there." She nodded toward the bar.

"Let's go over there and get a drink. See what happens." He held her hand and walked across the room.

As Mallory felt panic rise inside her, Roberto squeezed her fingers, stopped next to the director and ordered two sodas. He glanced at the circle of people the director was visiting with and, as Mallory was sure he'd hoped would happen, someone called his name as he was handing Mallory her drink.

"Roberto Castillo! How do you like NASCAR?"

He smiled. "So far so good." He drew Mallory along with him. "Though I wouldn't mind winning a race one of these days."

The group laughed.

"I'm sure you all know Mallory Dalton. She's starring in tonight's movie."

They all smiled and nodded.

"In fact," Roberto said, turning toward the director, "she's hoping to audition for your next movie."

Roberto was exactly what her career needed. Not Theo. She squeezed his hand back.

Then the director turned to her. *"Three Sisters?"*

She nodded. "If I can get an appointment with your casting director, yes."

"We'll make it happen."

The rest of the night went by in a blur. Roberto was a magnet, his mere presence drawing her into conversations with the kind of heavy hitters she never would've met on her own. She didn't know what she would've done without him.

"I ENJOYED SEEING YOU on the big screen," Roberto said as they left the Cinema Village theater. "You are good."

"Thank you," Mallory said. "We had a great team." They followed the red carpet back out to their limo. "I'm not ready to go home yet, though."

"What did you have in mind?"

"Let's go to the Avalon."

He glanced down at her, not sure if he heard correctly. The hot nightclub not too far from Madison Square Garden had loud music, big crowds and heavy drinking, the kind of place he might've frequented in his carousing days. "Why in the world would you want to go there? That place is nuts."

The paparazzi clicked photos. They climbed into the limo

and Roberto saw one photographer in particular following them on a scooter.

"Maybe we could go to the Blue Note. That's not far from here."

Jazz, nice atmosphere. What was she up to? She probably had no clue how hard it'd been for him to keep his distance from her tonight, but he'd managed. The last thing he wanted this late at night was to spend time in a sensual, sexy environment with her rubbing up against him.

"I have to fly out for the Texas race first thing in the morning," he said. "Let's take you home." He gave the address to the driver.

Mallory let go a long sigh as she settled back into her seat.

"What's going on?" he said.

"Nothing. I just feel wired."

"I think the last thing your agent would want is a bunch of photos of you with me at the Avalon."

Completely silent, she stared out the window. When they stopped at her apartment building, Roberto walked her to the door. He noticed the photographer from the theater drag his scooter onto the sidewalk down the block on the other side of the street.

"Thank you for coming tonight," Mallory said. "Thanks to you I might have that audition."

"My pleasure." And he meant it.

"Come up to my apartment," she whispered.

Oh, boy. Something had to have been in the water. "Not a good idea."

"So all that talk before in the limo?"

He didn't want to lie to her. "That photographer's been dogging our tail all night long."

"So?" She shrugged. "I'm getting used to it."

"That's not the point." He stepped away from her hoping the temptation would lessen. "I go up to your apartment and the whole city will know about it by morning."

She hooked her arms around his neck. "Maybe I don't care anymore."

"You'll care. So will your agent. And mine." He pulled her

arms down. "I'm not willing to take the heat for it." The statement couldn't have been further from the truth, but he didn't want to be responsible for damaging her reputation or her career.

Then he did one of the hardest things he'd ever had to do. He got back in the limo and had the driver take him home. Alone. Roberto Castillo turned down the offer of a beautiful, sexy woman's bed. A woman to whom he was immensely attracted. He never thought he'd live to see the day.

"IT'S OVER," Mallory said, yanking the ring off her finger and pressing it into her TV fiancé's hand. "I won't marry you."

"You're in love with someone else," the fiancé said, the acidic sounds of accusation tainting the sound of his voice. "Aren't you?"

"Yes," she whispered. "I suppose I am."

For several minutes, Roberto stood on the other side of the set, off-screen, watching the scene progress and waiting for his cue to enter the room so they could tape his third cameo appearance for *Racing Hearts*. Mallory was so good, so believable, the cameras and their operators, the assistant director, the grips, all seemed to disappear. It was as if he were a part of the scene, as if he were living this life.

"I can't believe it." The man chuckled and walked to the fake window on the set of her fake house. "All this time, you've been worried about me cheating on you, and what do you do? You cheat."

"I didn't cheat." She wrapped her arms around herself. "Not really. I only…kissed him once."

And what a kiss it had been. The type of happening that would make any person rethink an engagement. Roberto ran his hand over his mouth, remembering the way she'd felt, tasted, at that moment, and he was hit with the remembered scent of honey.

"Who is it?" The fiancé spun back around and grabbed Mallory angrily by the shoulders.

Roberto swallowed. *They are acting,* he told himself. *Acting.*

"Does it matter?" Mallory said.

"Hell, yes." He shook her.

If he hurts her, I'm going to kill him.

Mallory glanced into the man's face and looked torn, the exact emotion called for in the script. "His name's Roberto Castillo."

The fiancé narrowed his eyes. "You're kidding? *The* Roberto Castillo?"

She nodded, slowly.

He laughed again. "Are you nuts?"

Yes. Any woman would probably have to be completely insane to break off an engagement for the likes of Roberto.

"That man has the biggest playboy reputation in the entire racing industry. He'll break your heart."

Very likely.

"He's not like that," she said.

Yes, he is.

"He's kind and thoughtful."

Please.

"And he kisses engaged women." The man clenched his jaw, anger clearly setting in. "What was it like? When he kissed you?"

Perfection. And chaos. Together.

"It's not important." She turned away.

"Rocked your world, I suppose." The fiancé swung her back around. "You used to feel that way with me. Do you remember?"

The scene seemed to play out in slow motion before Roberto. The man pulled Mallory roughly into his arms, bent his head and pressed his lips to her mouth. *Son of a bitch.* The way the guy slanted his head there had to be tongue involved. *Was that really necessary?*

Roberto clenched his hands into fists. Fury raged through him like jet fuel. He couldn't breathe. He couldn't think. All he could do was watch, his feet frozen to the set.

Breathe. Slowly. He practiced the techniques he used to quiet his mind and relax his body during races. Then the man stepped away with a disappointed look on his face, and Roberto could finally swallow. *She doesn't love you, jerk.*

But she was a woman. In real life, would Mallory betray Roberto in some way? The question seemed to always be there, flittering at the edge of his consciousness. Would she turn on him as his own mother had?

"I won't take you back," the now ex-fiancé said. "You can cry and beg and get down on your knees. But I'll never take you back."

"I won't want you."

"We'll see." He walked out the door.

Roberto's cue. He glanced up and the assistant director raised a hand, silently signaling for him to enter the scene. Roberto opened the set door and stepped into Mallory's view. "Are you all right?" he asked.

She turned and ran into his arms. "It's over," she said. "I'm finally free."

"Cut. That's a wrap." The director came out of his box. "You were right, Mal. Ratings are up. Viewers love your character stepping out. Is it okay with you, Roberto, if we rewrite your upcoming cameos? A little sexier, more edgy?"

If it was what Mallory wanted, so be it. "No problem," he said.

"Good."

Then they were alone on the set. He closed his eyes and rested his cheek on top of her head. *This was crazy.*

Mallory hadn't moved from the circle of his arms. "Are you okay?" she asked against his chest, seeming to sense his turmoil.

"I'm good. Fine." He took a deep breath and forced his hands to his sides. "Ready for Mexico?"

"They cleared my schedule for me!" Excitement sparkled in her eyes. "And once I get through that audition, I'll be dying for a break."

He didn't deserve you. But then, neither do I.

CHAPTER ELEVEN

MALLORY COULDN'T REMEMBER ever having been this nervous. She'd been too naive to understand the importance of her first audition so many years ago, and most of her acting jobs, if she was honest with herself, hadn't been all that significant to her. But this one? She wanted this part. Even though she'd only be reading from one scene for this initial audition, she'd memorized every major scene. Every nuance of every line. If anything would help her break away from the America's Sweetheart stereotype, it'd be playing a recovering drug addict coming home only to ruin her sister's wedding.

The casting assistant knocked on the door and peeked inside the waiting room. "Mallory, they're ready for you."

Oh no. She was going to puke. Unable to find her voice, she could only follow the young woman into the conference room. There were several people she'd never met sitting around the table.

"Okay," the casting director said. "Mallory Dalton." She studied Mallory over the top of her reading glasses. "Are you the Mallory Dalton from *American Dream?* Little Amy Mitchell?"

Oh God. Now the woman was never going to recommend Mallory for this part. "Yep," she said, barely managing to squeak out the word.

"My daughter loved that show," she said, smiling. "Had a good run, didn't it?"

Mallory nodded and swallowed. *Talk. Fast. Or forever hold your peace.* "Seven years." She cleared her throat. "I've moved on, though. Did a small role in a romantic comedy released last week. And I've been a regular on the soap *Racing Hearts* for the last year."

"So you've got the sides, right?" She pointed toward the papers Mallory was holding in her hand.

This was the scene in the script Mallory would be reading. "Yeah, but I don't need them." She set them on the table.

"Okay, you're driving your sister crazy. Let's hear it." The casting director waved her hand, signaling an assistant to start recording the audition on a small video camera. "Whenever you're ready."

Mallory closed her eyes, took a deep breath and then signaled for the casting assistant to begin. Mallory stumbled over her first several words, but after that, she fell into her zone, reading her character's lines as she'd hoped. She finished and turned toward the group.

No one said anything.

The casting director sat back in her chair. "That was amazing. Are you familiar with any more of the script?"

Mallory nodded. "I've got most of the major scenes memorized."

The woman asked her to read part of another scene and another. Finally, she said, "Let's see you do number eight."

The most challenging one. The black moment for this character. Again, Mallory could feel it, her momentum building with every line. By the end, she knew she'd nailed it.

She turned to find the casting people glancing at one another. "Why do you want this part?" the casting director asked. "It's nothing like anything you've ever done."

"I'd like to be challenged for a change."

"Well, it's obvious you can act. But I have to be honest. The public still sees you as sweet little Amy Mitchell. They expect a certain type of character from Mallory Dalton. This part might be too much of a leap."

In other words, though she could act the part, possibly better than any other person under consideration, they still might not hire her.

"What if your *Racing Hearts* people tell you this movie's too gritty?" the casting director asked. "Then what?"

Showtime. Her heart pounded. "Then I'd quit the show."

She nodded thoughtfully. "Okay, Mallory, thank you. In a few weeks we'll be making callbacks for auditions with the director and producers. We'll let you know."

MEXICO CITY WAS HOT, congested, polluted, noisy and terribly smelly on occasion, but to Mallory it was promising to be the most amazing experience of her life. She was in a foreign country where everyone spoke Spanish and she got to go through customs for the first time in her life. Simply getting her passport stamped had been a thrill. A limo had met them at the airport, and now Mallory's gaze was glued out the window taking in the sights and sounds.

"You smile any wider and your face is going to crack," Roberto said.

She laughed. "This is so exciting."

"You think?" He glanced outside. "I guess the novelty has worn off for me."

"It looks like we're heading into the city."

"We are," Roberto said. "My home is in the Polanca district."

"I know where that is!" she said, thrilled that her study of the guidebook had actually come in handy. "You have a home there?"

"Mmm-hmm." He nodded. "Mostly for investment purposes."

"How many houses do you have?"

"A few," he said with a shrug. "New York, Paris, Mexico City and now Charlotte."

"They're all in the city?"

"I like the action." He grinned.

"Except for your country home in Argentina. Is that where you grew up?"

"*Dios,* no. I bought it more for my father than anything. He likes to stay busy. I was raised in a worker's shack on the large *estancia* where my father worked as a *gaucho.* Three rooms. Outside toilet. Spotty running water."

"Pretty rustic?"

"That's a nice way to put it."

"You didn't see your mother at all when you were little?"

"No." He glanced sideways at her. "Here's the gist of it. My mother's father was a high-profile banker. Very wealthy. My mother had a fling with my father when she was only sixteen and her family spent the next nine months covering it up."

"You make it sound as if she didn't want you at all."

"I don't think she did."

"What a terrible thing to say."

"Is it? Even if it's the truth?"

"She's your mother."

"She gave birth to me and handed me over to my father. He told me she died at my birth. Then when I was sixteen, I overheard my father mentioning her to a friend and found out she was still alive. That's when I ran away. To find her."

"All those years you thought she was dead. What happened when you met her?"

When he didn't answer right away, Mallory had the feeling it was something he'd tried to forget. "Let's just say I was very disappointed."

"She's why you hate women."

"I love women."

"No, you don't."

He tilted his head, studying her.

"I'm sorry. That was rude of me."

"No, not rude. Honest."

They drove off the freeway into what appeared to be an upscale combination residential and shopping area. Wide boulevards and large shade trees. Old but well-cared-for colonial buildings. With exclusive boutique hotels, trendy restaurants and designer shops, it looked like Rodeo Drive with a strong Mexican influence.

Their driver pulled up to a five-star chain hotel. "This is it." Roberto pointed out the window. "Let's get you settled in."

"I thought I was staying at your house."

"A hotel's better for appearances."

"I don't care about appearances. That's Theo's gig. If I stay in a chain hotel, it'll feel as if I could be in any big city in any country in the world. I want to experience the flavor of Mexico."

All that was true, but she also wanted the gossips to know she was ensconced in Roberto's home. That'd get the talk flowing. A momentary shot of guilt pinged through her when she thought about how this might affect Roberto's reputation, but he was a big boy. He could handle it.

"The Mexico experience." He studied her, clearly skeptical. "All right." He asked his driver to take them to his home, and a short time later, they drove up to a black, wrought-iron gate surrounding his property. The driver keyed in a security code, the gate opened and he drove through the main entrance, stopping on the circular drive in front of the house.

Mallory couldn't wait to see the inside. She quickly clambered out and glanced around. The home had a white stucco exterior with ornately carved wooden shutters and a red tiled roof. Gardens, shrubbery and grand shade trees surrounded the estate. Picturesque and traditional, the property looked exactly like the photos she'd seen in the guidebook of some of the country's old, well-kept homes.

"This is beautiful," she murmured.

He was watching her with a small smile on his face. "And you are easy to please."

"No. This is something."

"Come on, then. Let's go in."

Between the Spanish-tile flooring and large shade trees, the house was cool despite the heat of the day. The foyer opened to a great room with a huge fireplace against one wall. The back of the house was nearly all windows opening to a large veranda. From the architecture, intricate interior design, yet new appearance, it was obviously an old house that had been recently refurbished.

"I love this house," she said.

"It's pretty."

"It's gorgeous." She narrowed her eyes at him. "You didn't have anything to do with the decorating, did you?"

"Me?" He shook his head. "No. I have replaced a few things here and there, but I bought it as you see it, furnished and all."

The truth dawned on her. "You buy all your houses this way."

"Except for the country home in Argentina. In Charlotte I hired a decorator, gave her a budget and told her nothing too wild." He shrugged. "I rarely spend more than a few nights at any of them, so as long as they have a more homey appearance than a hotel room, I'm happy."

"You never stay with the rest of the drivers in motor homes at the tracks, do you?"

"No."

"Why not?"

He stood there, silent for a moment. "Too close of quarters for my taste."

He grabbed her bags, leaving his by the door, and she followed him down a long hall and into a large bedroom. The room had an intense, rich feel, with heavy bedspreads and drapes, dark mahogany furniture and the walls painted a dark red. He'd set her suitcases down next to the massive king-size four-poster bed when their driver came to the door, carrying Roberto's suitcase.

"Where would you like bag your, Mr. Castillo?"

"Set it in my closet, thank you, Carlos."

The driver walked past Mallory, opened the closet door, set Roberto's suitcase down and then left.

Taken by surprise, Mallory glanced around. "So this is your bedroom?"

"*Sí.*" He wouldn't take his eyes off her. "When you said no hotel, I assumed this is what you wanted." He walked toward her, too close. "It's about time, isn't it, *querida?* For you and I to make this official?"

That option got more and more tempting every moment they spent together, but, she told herself, she'd come to Mexico for appearances only.

"If by that you mean sleeping together—" she stepped back, putting some space between them "—then no. I'd like a guest bedroom, please." She made a move toward the hall, but he stopped her with a hand on her arm.

"Are you sure?" His thumb traced circles on her skin.

"If I change my mind, I'll know where to find you."

He laughed and took her bags across the hall. "Here you are, then. In the guest bedroom."

This room was smaller than Roberto's and decorated in yellows, but with similar rich fabrics and furniture. "Thank you."

"I'm not sure what game you are playing, Mallory." He turned toward her and his smile all but disappeared. "But I'll play along. For now."

THE MEXICO CITY TRACK was a flat, alternating-turn course as opposed to the all left-turn, oval tracks with banked turns characteristic of most NASCAR races. This track had been designed to easily convert from a four-turn oval into a seventeen-turn course or anything in between. The charity race on Sunday was set to be a cross between the two extremes with eight turns.

"I don't know much about this type of road race," Mallory said.

"That's okay," Roberto replied. "You'll pick it up quickly. This is a slower kind of race because of all the turns. You can't see the whole track, so watch the screens."

The sun was bright and hot as he walked side by side with her to his car for the first of his practice runs. Expectation thrummed through him, something he hadn't felt for a long time. Part of the excitement had to do with running more of his kind of race, but much of it had to do with Mallory being here. This was the first time she'd come to practice or qualifying, to anything other than his actual races, and her request to accompany him this afternoon had pleased him on some primal, gut level.

That's a mistake, something inside him cautioned, *to expect too much from a woman.* They always seemed to disappoint.

She's why you hate women.

Mallory's comment about his mother had haunted Roberto from the time it had slipped from her lips yesterday afternoon. Why would she say that? Was it true? Had his mother had such an impact on him that he was taking his shots at every woman?

End the relationship before she did. He'd had that thought more times than he could count these past years. Maybe he didn't so much hate women as fear them, their betrayals and their rejections.

But Mallory, he reminded himself, was not like other women.

He succumbed to a sudden urge, tilted her face toward him and kissed her gently. A quick peck didn't come close to what he wanted from her, but it would have to do. "I'm glad you came to Mexico with me."

"Roberto!" Harry was yelling for him. "Get a move on. We're ready for practice."

Roberto climbed inside his No. 507 car and glanced over at Mallory.

"Good luck," she mouthed while holding two thumbs up, and then he was out on the track.

"How's it feel?" Harry asked.

"Loose," Roberto said.

"She'll tighten up."

Roberto gained speed and, yes, he got to make a right turn.

"Bet that felt good." Harry laughed.

"Damn right it did," Roberto said. "First one of those in a long time."

They went through several adjustments. Roberto was still getting the hang of how to communicate the exact changes he needed on the car. By the last of the practice runs, they were ready for qualifying.

Several hours later, Roberto knew he had a good qualifying run even before Harry said anything.

"Hot diggity!" Harry yelled. "You just broke the track record for qualifying."

"What did I do?"

"75.067 mph!"

That was slow compared to a regular NASCAR track, but with eight turns—two of them hairpin—and only a couple of short straightaways, there was no way a stock car could come close to their normal speeds of 180 miles an hour. Hell, the last time he'd raced this track with an open-wheel, Roberto had averaged somewhere around only 115 miles an hour.

"That's going to get you the pole position, Roberto."

"It better." This was his track. This might be a charity event, but everyone expected him to win. *He* expected to win.

CHAPTER TWELVE

THAT NIGHT, after qualifying, the organizers of the charity race benefiting Mexican children battling cancer put on a party for the participating drivers. Much to Roberto's consternation, Mallory wore the bright, floral-print dress that he'd picked out and had delivered to her in Charlotte for this trip.

He was beginning to wish he'd never gone on that spur-of-the-moment shopping excursion. She was looking too damned good. Not because he cared what other men were thinking, but because he could barely think when he was around her. Especially tonight. The dress had only one shoulder strap and he found his gaze continually drawn to her bare shoulder.

Finally, wanting no longer to be tempted by the sight of her, he whispered in her ear, "Let's go home." Then he could lock himself in his bedroom and try to sleep.

"Right now?" she said, her disappointment evident. "What about dessert?"

They'd just finished a main entrée of cilantro and lime grilled fish with a mango chutney, but if it was up to him, he'd get to enjoy something—someone—other than food as sweets. In private. Instead, he said, "I'm tired."

They slipped quietly away from the group and headed to Roberto's car. Tonight, he'd driven himself. They'd almost made it to his house when Mallory pointed at a plain-looking, glass-fronted building and exclaimed, "The Bar Fly! Pull over!"

"Figures." Chuckling, he parked at the curb in the nearest open spot.

She spun toward him. "I read about that place. They have a Cuban band that plays the best salsa and merengue music in town."

"I know. I have been there. Many times." He raised his eyebrows at her. "Hot, spicy dancing. There will be people with cameras, they will see us and they will publish pictures."

"I know," she said.

"Mallory, what—" First the casino, then Mexico. Finally, he figured it out. "We have been at cross-purposes all this time, *sí?*"

"I'm sure I don't know what you mean." She sounded innocent, but he suddenly knew better.

"*My* agent loves your American Sweetheart persona. Your agent fights tooth and nail to maintain it. But *you?*" He paused, watching the way the pale light of the streetlamps illuminated her face. "You want it gone, don't you?"

She looked down and away for a moment, then she scrunched up her mouth and glanced back at him. "Like a bad rash."

He laughed. He was going to be in so much trouble with Patricia and the Grossos when this made it back to the States. "Well," he said, "can you dance?"

"A little." She glanced expectantly at him. "I had to take lessons years ago for a part, so I'm a bit rusty. We didn't practice any Latin dances, but I'm a fast learner. Can we go anyway?"

"Absolutely. Let's go trash your reputation." He'd worry about the consequences to his own tomorrow. The music was already in full swing and the dance floor crowded by the time they went inside. "Do you want a drink?" he asked.

"No, thanks."

"Then let's go." He grabbed her hand and swung her onto the tiny dance floor. "Salsa, anyone?"

She stepped into his embrace and started to move. The beat was contagious. In no time, he was spinning her, she was spinning him, but when he started messing with funky arm positioning, she slowed him down. "Whoa, whoa, whoa. You're moving too fast for me."

"You are doing great." He drew her close so they could talk. A woman from a nearby table snapped a picture of them.

Roberto's instinctive reaction was to protect Mallory, so he swung her around, blocking the view. Then he remembered she wanted this publicity, and he pulled her closer. "How far do you want to go with this?"

"With what?"

"Showing the not-so-sweet side of Mallory Dalton."

"What did you have in mind?"

He slid his hands lower, and tugged her so close there wasn't a slice of air between them. Then he bent toward her mouth, their noses touching. "How's that?"

"That'll do some damage," she whispered, closing her eyes. She turned to liquid fire in his arms.

He spun her around and held her in that position, their profiles clear enough to anyone paying attention. Several flashes went off, and one individual raised a cell phone as if taking a video. There was little doubt that was going to make it on to the Internet. Roberto quickly spun her away from him. It was a damned good thing they were in a crowded room, otherwise he'd have her out of that dress in seconds.

When she looked up at him, her eyes were dark. "Who taught you to dance like this?" she whispered in his ear.

"My father. The *gauchos* love to kick it up on a Friday night. They haul out their instruments. Sip on some tequila. If they are lucky, a few wives or girlfriends stop by. It's cheap entertainment."

The salsa song slowed and the band rolled into a merengue. She glanced around, a little panicked. "I don't think I can do this one."

"If you can walk, you can merengue." He took a few quick steps, swinging his hips from side to side. "All you have to do is keep your feet stepping to the beat." He stepped across the dance floor. "One-two, one-two. That's all there is to it. Watch my chest."

Forget his chest. Mallory could barely keep her eyes off the way he swung his hips. She'd never seen a man move that smoothly, and a man had never, never held her the way he did on this dance floor. No wonder every woman wanted her hands on him.

"*Querida,* where are you?" he said, reaching for her. He kept some distance between them so they could each move freely.

After only a minute or two, he pulled her closer. "You are a natural. Are you sure you aren't Latina?"

She laughed. But there was something about this country—the music, the food, the language—that spoke to her. "Do I look Latina?"

"Actually, yes."

"Sorry. Mostly English and Norwegian. My dark coloring came from a Greek grandmother."

"That explains it, then."

After several more songs, they each sucked down a bottle of water and headed back to the dance floor. Roberto held her close for a slow one. She laid her head on his shoulder, and he tightened his hand at the small of her back, bringing their mid-sections into intimate contact. She closed her eyes and their bodies swayed together. He led so well that her body predicted his movements before her mind comprehended where she was going.

"You could dance all night, couldn't you?" he whispered.

"With you, yes." She glanced at him. He made her feel so vibrant and alive, but dark circles had appeared under his eyes. "You're tired, aren't you?"

He nodded. "*Sí,* the day is catching up to me."

"Let's go, then." She took his hand and led him outside.

They arrived at Roberto's house less than ten minutes later. He sat down on the couch, while she went into the kitchen to get them both some water. By the time she came back, he'd kicked off his shoes and jacket and unbuttoned his shirt. He was lying on the couch and his eyes were closed. He grabbed her hand the moment she came close. "Sit here with me."

"I don't think—"

"Don't think. Please." He pulled her down alongside him.

"Dancing is one thing," she whispered. "This is—"

"Shh." He wrapped both his arms around her, buried his face in her hair and seemed to breath her in. "I had a good day," he whispered. "An even better night."

"Me, too." It *had* been a good night. She smiled. One of her best ever. There was one thing that would make this a perfect night. One perfect kiss. Nothing more, nothing less.

She snuggled up along his side, rested her cheek against his chest and ran her hand along his arm. In truth, she wanted to run her hands under his shirt and along his warm skin… But that would be too much, too soon.

She trailed her fingertips along his stomach, moved higher. His chest rose and fell in a measured, steady rhythm. His arms went completely lax. "Roberto?"

No response. Only slow, quiet breaths.

He was asleep. She smiled. *The* Roberto Castillo had a willing woman in his arms and he'd fallen asleep. But then her smile waned as a thought occurred to her. For Roberto, a night like this was only one of countless good nights with countless other women. She was one of many. With many more women to come.

He'd been sweet and accommodating tonight, but she couldn't delude herself into thinking he actually cared about her for more than the moment, more than all the rest of the women who had come in and out of his life.

ROBERTO PULLED onto pit road and quickly braked to a stop. The crew dashed to and fro around the car. *Let's go! Let's go!* It seemed to be taking forever. He sat up to see who the hell was changing his left front tire. The man glanced over the fender and grinned at him.

Papá? How had his father gotten here?

Roberto's eyes snapped open to blackness, cut only by a single slice of moonlight. *Where the hell?* Then he remembered. Mexico. His home. His couch. Mallory. The blissful warmth of her body ran the length of his side. He turned his head and ran his cheek along the silky softness of her hair and became cognizant of the position of his right arm, the way it was wrapped around her and his hand, resting at her side, inches from her heart.

Two minutes to enjoy this, he told himself, and then he would carry her to her bed. And leave her there. Two minutes to lie here and imagine what her bare skin would feel like, her back, her side, her tummy. Two minutes to imagine what it would be like to roll over with her and lose himself inside her warmth.

Ay, yi, yi.

His traitorous, evil arm searched for the zipper to her dress and inched it down. *If she wakes, game's over.* She didn't. The hand attached to that wayward arm slipped between the open folds of fabric and pressed against her skin, so warm it almost burned. Still not awake.

Perfect. She was perfect. He sucked in a breath and clenched his jaw. And she was still sound asleep.

Wrapping his arm around her, he shifted to his side, drawing her close to him. He leaned over her, let the look of her, eyes closed, bare neck gleaming up at him, lips slightly parted, hair splayed out behind her head, brand his memory.

He'd never wanted a woman as much as he wanted Mallory in this moment. And never, never had he exercised this level of restraint. *Wake up. Stop me.* Slowly, he bent his head and ran a trail of kisses from one gorgeous shoulder, over a collarbone, across her chest to rest at the other shoulder. *Wake up. Before I can't stop.* He pressed his face into her neck and kissed her jaw, the corner of her mouth, her lips.

And then her mouth fully opened and she was kissing him back. Feverishly. Her hands, restless and urgent, ran under his shirt, then along his side and up his neck. Her fingers delved into his hair and Roberto had a momentary urge to pull back. Too close. She was too close. But as he pressed back against her hand, she lifted her head, deepening their kiss.

No, not close enough. She could have his head on a silver platter for all he cared. He groaned, giving in.

Immediately, as if the sound had brought her fully aware, she tensed. And then, wide-eyed, shoved her hands against his chest. "I can't do this."

"Yes, you can."

"No." She pushed again and jumped up, only to have her dress, now partially unzipped, slip nearly to her waist. "Oh my God." She yanked up the fabric. "You nearly undressed me!"

"You are a very sound sleeper."

"And if I hadn't woken up?"

His answer must've shown on his face.

She snatched a book from the coffee table, threw it at him and stalked down the hall. "You're an animal!" she said over her shoulder.

Chuckling, he yelled back at her, "And *you* are all show and no action!" He flopped back against the couch, and his smile disappeared as his ache for her heightened to outright pain. "America's Sweetheart is no fun at all," he said. But he knew it wasn't true. Shoving his fingers through his hair, he remembered the way she'd touched him, possessed him.

Animal was right. Caged to boot.

MALLORY SHUT the bedroom door and leaned back against the cold, hard wood, hoping to shock her body out of the wonderfully heated place it so very much wanted to stay. She was panting, feral and crazed, like the animal she'd called him.

So he thought America's Sweetheart was no fun, eh? If he only knew. When she'd first woken up, felt his mouth against her lips, her body, already stoked by his touch, had burst into flames. If she'd been naked, there was no doubt in her mind what would've happened next.

All show and no action. On that, though, he was dead-on. So what was stopping her? She heard him coming down the hall. *Don't stop. Stop. Oh, God, don't stop.*

He stopped. She could feel his presence on the other side of the door. She held her breath. If he knocked, if he turned the knob, they'd be right back where they started and, this time, she wasn't sure she could summon the willpower to push him away.

Then she heard his footsteps continue into his own room, the door close and the sound of water running. A shower? She chuckled softly in the darkness. There probably wasn't enough cold water in all of Mexico to dampen her need. She hoped he had better luck.

"WELL, I HOPE you're happy," Patricia said, sounding uncharacteristically disheartened. "You've really done it this time."

"What's that?" Roberto said, but he had a feeling he already knew what this phone call was all about. She happened to catch him on his cell phone alone in the kitchen of his Mexico City home. Mallory had woken up a short while ago and was now taking a shower.

"Theo's calling off the Mallory deal. Enjoy what's left of your Mexico trip because when she gets home, I wouldn't put it past him to throw a chastity belt on her and lock her in an ivory tower."

As if Mallory had absolutely nothing to say about it. If Theo Stein was, at this moment, in front of Roberto, he would've punched the man right between the eyes. "I'm going to wager that pictures of us dancing at the Bar Fly were published somewhere."

"Try everywhere. There's even a video circulating showing you grabbing her butt. What were you thinking?"

That what Mallory needed from him was more important than what he needed from her.

"They've interviewed one of your staff who claims Mallory's staying at your house." When he still didn't say anything, she sighed. "Please, please say she's not staying with you." Another pause. "Oh, for God's sake, Roberto. What do you expect from me, freaking miracles? I don't think I can damage-control this one."

"How bad is it?"

"This heading pretty much sums it up—Is Racing's Playboy Turning America's Sweetheart Sour?"

He chuckled. "South of the border, they seem to like the match." He tossed aside the entertainment section of a Mexico City newspaper showing the picture of him intimately dancing with Mallory. The heading read True Love At Last?

He had to admit the feelings he had for Mallory were different from what he'd felt for any other woman and confusing. But love? He was fairly certain he was incapable.

"You're dead in the water," Patricia said.

"Are you saying the Grossos won't renew my contract?"

"They'll have grounds, that's for sure. You're lucky they're busy with their daughter's wedding, but they'll eventually hear about it. And when they do, I'm going to guess you'll be renewed or cut loose based solely on your driving record."

"That isn't so bad, is it?"

"As long as you're winning," Patricia said. "Tell me this. Is she worth it?"

That, unfortunately, was yet to be decided.

CHAPTER THIRTEEN

THE MEXICO CITY RACE was like nothing Mallory had ever seen before and she'd been to a lot of different kinds of races through the years with her family. With so many turns and zero banking, the Mexico City track was slower than most, but fraught with danger. At nearly every turn—and it was strange to have right turns—it seemed cars either hit or had near misses, causing spinouts and accidents. She sat on the war wagon with Harry, biting her nails and wringing her hands for most of the race.

Roberto was confident. He'd run in first place for much of the race and it seemed to be his day. Still, every time a car nudged him, she tensed. So did he. She could hear it in his voice.

"Two to go," Roberto's spotter announced over the headset.

Silence. Harry didn't want to say anything that might jinx them and neither did Roberto. He was advancing on a couple slower cars, getting ready to lap them.

"Híjole!" Roberto said.

The drivers crashed in front of him.

"Stay inside," his spotter said. "Get out of there."

Roberto was forced to cut the corner and head straight through the dirt to get back onto the track. It looked as if one of the other cars barely clipped his left rear fender, but he got back on the track still in first place.

"One to go," the spotter said.

After a few turns, Roberto said quickly, "She doesn't feel right."

"Talk to me," Harry said.

"Doesn't matter, does it?" Roberto snapped. "I can't pit."

Mallory watched in horror as the second- and third-place cars passed Roberto and he only growled across the radio.

"Dammit!" Mallory said as the cars crossed the finish line.

Roberto had finished in third when he'd dominated all day. It should have been his race. It would have been, if not for that last spinout in front of him.

Disheartened, Roberto's team headed back to the garage. Roberto turned his car into the area and jumped out only to have a reporter thrust a microphone in his face. Mallory stood back, watching, feeling for him.

"Third." A woman in the crowd behind Mallory muttered the word with disdain.

Mallory clenched her jaw. Roberto had driven the best he could. He couldn't help it that the car had started giving him problems after avoiding that crash. No other driver could've done better. Feeling protective, Mallory spun around, ready to take on the woman.

A middle-aged woman, dripping with heavy gold jewelry, dressed in a red silk shirt and a wide-brimmed hat, came stalking into the garage. "You would think he could have done better on a road course."

"Who are you?" She wasn't letting this bit—person near Roberto.

The woman flipped off her large sunglasses, revealing large, pretty brown eyes, framed with heavy eyeliner. "Who are you?"

"Mallory Dalton." She took a step to the left, putting herself directly in the woman's path.

"Ah. America's Sweetheart." She nodded. "You are a NASCAR fan, aren't you?"

"Yes."

"Why is that?"

"Why am I a NASCAR fan?"

The woman nodded.

What a silly question. "I don't know," Mallory said. "I grew up with it. I've always loved to watch the races."

"That's not a particularly good reason. Have you ever seen my son race open-wheel?"

"I'm not sure. Who's your son?"

"Over there." The woman smiled. "The one you are protecting. From me."

"Roberto's mother." Mallory felt her cheeks turn hot with embarrassment. "I'm sorry."

"Camila Franco." The woman held out her hand. "And don't be sorry. It's not the first time he's needed protection from me. I can't help it. I hate it when he drives so poorly."

"He ran a good race today."

"He can do better. He should have won."

"Yes, I should have." Roberto's voice, slow and deep, sounded from behind Mallory. "But that's the interesting thing about stock cars." He put his hand on Mallory's right shoulder and squeezed. "You never know what's going to happen."

"Well." Camila shrugged. "I came to your race, and I wanted you to know I was here. That's all."

"*Gracias, Madre.* Maybe next time, you'll actually enjoy yourself."

"Hmm." She raised her eyebrows. "Try winning for a change." She spun around and walked away.

"I'm sorry," Mallory said, glancing at him. "I know she's your mother, but she was…"

"Rude?"

Mallory nodded.

"That's because I didn't win."

Of all the… Mallory looked after Camila, ready to take that woman on. How could she call herself a mother?

Roberto laughed. "It's okay. I'm used to her."

"You shouldn't have to get used to that. It's bad enough you have to take criticism from your car owners, crew chief, fans. Your mother should be your…your…"

"Champion? Advocate?" He paused. "Defender?"

"Yes." It was clear he'd never had a woman play that role in his life.

"That's why I have you." At that moment, he looked vulnerable and uncertain, nothing like a cynical playboy he wanted everyone to see.

"My parents are having a fortieth anniversary party in Dover," she said. Her invitation was going to sound as if it were coming out of nowhere, but he deserved to be a part of a family, and hers, with all its faults, was a good one. "I know it's not until June, but will you come?"

"I'd love to." He grabbed her hand and headed toward the driver's airstrip. "Now, come. Let's go home."

RICHMOND. Another short track.

Roberto yanked his Molloy Cycle cap lower over his brow as he headed toward the garage on race day, feeling relatively comfortable with how he'd performed in practice laps and qualifying. But since there hadn't been forty-two other cars on the track with him at a time, his qualifying position wouldn't be a clear indicator of how he'd do during the actual race. Still, his car was running well and, despite not winning in Mexico, his confidence was improving. He'd done all right at last week's Talladega race, but that'd been a superspeedway.

Dammit. He wished Mallory was here. She hadn't come to Phoenix or Talladega, either. First, her agent had booked some audition and then several photo shoots at the last minute, making it impossible for her to leave Manhattan. Roberto hadn't said anything about Patricia's phone call. Mallory needed to come to terms with Theo on her own.

He, on the other hand, still needed help figuring out his short track strategy. There was no point in talking to Nathan; the man had bigger problems on his mind. Dean and Patsy had been clearly preoccupied with the search for Gina. He'd about talked Harry Skelly's ear off, and that hadn't seemed to help.

That left Kent. The other driver was no doubt thinking about the possibility of finding his twin sister, but Roberto had a feeling he might welcome the distraction. It was time to bite the bullet once and for all.

Roberto found Kent sitting next to Perry Noble, his crew chief, in their garage. Kent glanced at him, but didn't bother saying anything.

"Can I talk to you?" Roberto said.

Kent cocked his head. "That depends."

"I'll let you guys chat." Perry stood and headed outside into the bright sunlight.

Roberto hesitated, framing his thoughts and glancing around the garage. Several team members were going about their business, but no one was paying any particular attention to him. "I'm not sure how to say this," he said to Kent.

"In English would be nice."

Roberto stifled a nasty response. In truth, it was his fault he and Kent had started off on bad footing. Roberto was going to have to make the first move to reconcile.

"Look, we got off on a rocky start this season."

"Is that your idea of an apology?"

"I guess so."

"Well, then, I guess it's accepted." Kent gulped down some water.

"That's not all. Bristol. Martinsville. I'm… I…" Roberto said, faltering.

"Well, I'll be damned." Kent chuckled. "You need my help, don't you?"

Roberto nodded. He was a big enough man. He could admit his failings. "Yes. I do need your help."

"Never thought I'd see the day." Kent slapped his leg. "Hey, everybody!" Kent yelled to everyone in the garage. They quieted and turned toward the younger Grosso.

Híjole! Roberto looked outside. Even Perry had turned his head to listen to what Kent was saying.

"Roberto asked for my help," Kent said, and the entire garage erupted in laughter. "Should I give it to him?"

"Yes!" came the resounded response.

With a smile on his face, Kent turned to Roberto.

"I suppose I deserved that," Roberto said.

Kent turned serious. "Okay, what do you want to know?"

"WHAT DO YOU SAY we go out to dinner?" Theo said as Mallory left the midtown studio with him.

She glanced at her watch. The Richmond race began a half an hour ago. If she went directly home from the photo shoot, she could still catch most of it on TV.

"You don't have plans, right?"

Before this moment, she'd been suspicious he'd scheduled this shoot for a *Racing Hearts* promo on a weekend so she'd have to miss being in Richmond for the Saturday-night race, but now it was obvious. She and Theo had never, in the ten years she'd been working with him, been out to dinner on a weekend.

"Why are you doing this?" she asked.

"Doing what?"

"Purposefully keeping me away from Roberto's races."

He chuckled. "Okay, you caught me."

"Theo, it's not funny." She stepped toward the curb and flagged down a cab. "I don't appreciate being manipulated."

"Mallory, we need to talk."

She glanced back. He was still the best agent in town, but she had a message on her cell phone calling her back to her second audition for *Three Sisters* and this one would be with the movie director and the producers. Should she burn her Theo bridge or continue tiptoeing across? Dammit. Probably best to wait until she had the job in hand.

"Fine, let's talk on my way home." She opened the back door to the taxi, climbed in and gave the driver her Chelsea address. "You've got a few blocks to speak your mind."

He climbed in next to her and slammed the door. "I know you went around me and auditioned for *Three Sisters* on your own." At her silent, questioning look, he explained, "People talk. Everyone knows everyone else in this industry."

"I'm sorry, Theo, but I want that part."

"And if you get it, you might lose the romantic comedy. The studio called me the other day. They wanted to make sure we understand that they want light, fresh and funny. They want you the way you are, not new and improved. And all this Roberto

Castillo press is coloring your image. He's no longer useful to us. Overall, he's done more damage than good."

"I don't care. I like being with him."

"Well, that's become very obvious. You need to stop seeing him."

Stop seeing Roberto. The thought made her stomach flip-flop. "We're contracted for two more cameos together. I'm going to have to continue to see him."

"The cameos are one thing. Seeing him on your own time is different. Mallory, I didn't want to go here, but I'm trying to protect you."

"From what?"

"Yourself."

She stared at him.

"I've known you for a long time, sweetheart."

She hated it when he sounded like a father.

"In fact, when I first met you, you were a little girl."

She'd been twenty.

"I've seen you mature and grow into a lovely young woman. How you've maintained your innocence in this business is beyond me, but you have. Maybe I can take a little credit for that, being picky with the roles you've taken."

It was everything she could do to keep her mouth shut.

"Mostly, though, I think it's who you are. You've always made good choices with the men you've dated. Clean-cut, respectful, mature."

And boring.

"The Mallory Dalton I know doesn't have casual relationships."

She hadn't had much in terms of relationships. Period.

"I was hoping we could keep this thing with Roberto low-key, but you're getting drawn in way too deep. Think about it. With your head. Not your heart. If you think you mean anything to that man, you're kidding yourself."

That was it. "Why would you say that?"

"This is Roberto Castillo we're talking about. Remember? This man does not get serious with women. He uses women. And then he discards them like…flat champagne. The only reason he agreed to see you is because the relationship benefited him. When he's through with you, when he's taken all he can from his association with you, he'll drop you so fast your head will spin."

"I don't believe that."

"I don't know what game he's playing, but he's a man, Mallory. I know what he's thinking, and it's not sweet and it's not pretty." Theo shook his head. "Have you slept with him yet?"

"That's none of your business."

He studied her face. "You haven't. I'd bet money on it. And all I can say is don't. Trust me. Once you have sex with that man—and don't delude yourself into thinking you'd be making love, it would be sex, plain and simple—you become another conquest. One more name tacked on to a long list of women."

"He's different," she whispered. "He's a different man today."

"And you believe that because you're Mallory Dalton." He stated the fact like an insult, and then he released a heavy sigh as the taxi rolled to a stop at a red light. "Do yourself a favor, Mallory. Finish your cameos and then finish with Roberto. Before he finishes with you." He climbed out of the cab and slammed the door.

Mallory watched Theo head to the curb and walk back the way they'd come. His words hung there, swinging back and forth inside the cab like the blade of a sharp knife, cutting her to bits. She felt raw, bruised and bloodied. She couldn't deny that Theo could be right. She did have a tendency to think the best of people, and she'd only met Roberto two short months ago. How well could she really know the man?

There was no disputing that his past included a long line of women, famous and infamous, all gorgeous, all fast and loose, and a man didn't change overnight.

Disheartened, Mallory climbed out of the cab and took the elevator to her apartment. She kicked off her shoes, turned on the TV, slumped back onto the big sectional sofa and watched the rest of the race in a daze. Every time she heard the sound of Roberto's voice or the announcers mention his name, it felt as if a vice had tightened on her heart.

In postrace interviews, she watched Payton Reese, the NSN reporter speaking with his brother-in-law, Justin Murphy, and caught a background glimpse of Rachel Reese, Payton's very pregnant wife and Justin's sister, smiling and congratulating the team. It was sad, really. Having spent hours at the tracks with Roberto, she'd met so many of these people. He'd opened up the NASCAR world to her, and, when all of this was over, she was going to miss it.

The spotlight turned to another announcer interviewing drivers in the garage area, and Roberto and Kent popped up on the screen. Roberto looked happy, content with the outcome of today's race. He'd finished eighth, his best finish so far, other than Mexico, in his first NASCAR season.

How could this man be using her? But, then, maybe that was all part of his game. No one could argue that Roberto Castillo knew what women wanted.

"So what's going on with you two today?" the announcer asked.

Kent slapped Roberto on the back. "He figured it out, that's what."

Roberto shook his head. "Kent's one of the best drivers out there. I'm glad to be on his team."

They went on to discuss various turning points in the race, but Mallory barely heard the words. She could only watch Roberto on the TV screen. Now that she knew him, understood he hated the necessary interviewing gigs, his habits were easy to decipher, like his eyebrow arching. The question the reporter had asked was probably silly or inappropriate. Or the way Roberto rubbed his cheek with the back of his left hand, meaning he was getting impatient with the reporter and wanted to move on. The reporter ended the interview and Roberto disappeared.

She might think she knew him, that she could read his body language, but did she? Did she really know Roberto Castillo?

He uses women. And then he discards them like flat champagne.

They'd be taping Roberto's fourth cameo for *Racing Hearts* on Tuesday. He'd be coming back to the New York studio this time, and he didn't know this yet, but it was a bedroom scene, both of them under the sheets, supposedly naked and having just made love. And for the first time in her acting career, Mallory wondered how she was going to pull off a scene.

"TO CARGILL-GROSSO!" Kent held up a frosty can of beer and toasted the day's performance.

"You guys did an awesome job!" Roberto praised their teams.

"Cheers!" Both Roberto's and Kent's teams raised their beers in a toast.

"I'm proud of you guys," Dean said.

"Me, too," Patsy added with a big smile, hugging Kent and then making the rounds.

Roberto clanked his water bottle against Kent's beer can and then took a long chug. He'd be off on his private jet to his Manhattan apartment and Kent, Dean and Patsy would be on the Cargill-Grosso Racing plane heading back with the rest of their team, but with the adrenaline of the race running through the team, they'd all decided a quick celebration was in order.

"At first, I wasn't so sure Mom and Dad were making the right decision in signing you on with us," Kent said. "But now…"

"Now?" Roberto grinned.

"For what it's worth," Kent said, slamming down his empty can of beer, "I'm glad you're here."

"Me, too."

"In fact, I think it's high time you give up your hotels and stay in a motor home at the next track. Like the rest of us lowly drivers. What do you think?"

"You going to bring me room service?"

Kent grinned. "Sure, why not? Breakfast in bed. Fresh towels. Turn down your sheets."

"Little chocolates on my pillow."

"Now that's pushing it." Kent shook his head.

For the first time since signing on with the Grossos, Roberto felt a part of these teams, more than he'd ever felt in open-wheel racing. And a new friend was certainly an outcome he'd never expected in coming to NASCAR.

Kent glanced up. "Uh-oh." Dean and Patsy were heading toward Roberto. "They look pretty pissed off. What'd you do?"

Mexico. "I'll see you later, Kent." He met the Grossos halfway.

"Roberto, we need to talk," Dean said. "I don't know what the hell you're doing, but your Mallory Dalton plan appears to be backfiring."

"Dean, let me talk to him," Patsy said, taking Roberto's arm and drawing him away from the group. "That charity event in Mexico City was an opportunity for you to shine from a public-image standpoint. And instead," she said, stopping and glancing around the garage, "some very disturbing pictures were published of you and Mallory Dalton dancing. Honestly, I wouldn't have expected something like that from her."

What could Roberto say?

"You and Kent are the most visible faces of Cargill-Grosso Racing. What you two do reflects on all of us."

"I understand that."

"Do you? Really?" She studied him. "I have to admit, Dean cares more about your driving record. I'm the one who insisted on you cleaning up your image."

He might've guessed that.

"Do you know why?"

"Not really, no."

"Because when I'm in the grocery store, the mall or the gas station and my neighbors look at me and whisper to each other, I'd like to hold my head up high and trust that my team hasn't given them anything to gossip about."

Roberto looked away.

"As long as you're running well in races, Roberto, you'll get your contract for next year, but I'd like to think you're a man who honors his promises."

CHAPTER FOURTEEN

ROBERTO THREW the script down on his dressing room table. Mallory. In bed. With him. Nearly naked. When the director had said they'd be rewriting Roberto's cameos he hadn't been kidding. Roberto's scenes were supposed to be portraying him as a knight in shining armor. Instead, they were reinforcing his playboy image. Not that Roberto really cared.

Except for the part where the cast members and entire crew would be looking on. And the fact that Patricia was going to hit the roof if she saw this episode. And Patsy? Hell, he didn't even want to think about her reaction.

But this was what Mallory wanted, what she felt she needed for her career. How could he disappoint her? He couldn't. That was all there was to it.

Preoccupied, he paced back and forth, waiting to get called onto the set. Running late today, he'd gotten to the studio with no time to search for Mallory, and he hadn't seen her for more than two weeks.

The seduction scene was to take place in a quiet bar, and then it was up to his supposed hotel room. Before he knew it, he found himself sitting at a fake bar, nursing a fake drink and the director had started taping. The camera was to zoom in on him. A soft jazz piano sounded in the background.

From the fringe of darkness at the edge of the set, Mallory appeared. He watched her walking toward him. It had been interesting to see how her character had evolved over the past few months, maybe not to the degree the real Mallory had, but there were still obvious changes, like the dress she was wearing. It was royal blue and fitted. She looked confident and poised. Sexy.

When she came to the bar, he said softly, "I thought you might be here tonight."

She glanced up, her deer-in-the-headlights look slowly transforming into one of quiet joy. God, she was good. "I'm glad you were thinking. About me." She slid into the seat next to him.

"Are you staying at this hotel?"

"No," she said.

"No?" He looked surprised, innocent. The question of what she was doing there hung unspoken between them as the look on her face changed from lighthearted playfulness to sultry suggestion. "Are you?"

"Yes," he said, nearly forgetting his lines. "And I hate sleeping alone."

"Maybe tonight you don't have to."

"Room 2157," he whispered, getting very turned on. "I'll meet you there." He finished his drink and left the lounge.

"Cut. That was perfect," the director said. "Hotel room, people. I'm sure Roberto's on a tight schedule!"

"Mr. Castillo?" The wardrobe lady nabbed him at the hotel room set. "We need you in these." She handed him a pair of white basketball shorts.

Without a word, Mallory disappeared into her dressing room.

Dios. He was in trouble. He went into a dressing room, ditched his clothes for the shorts and put a robe on before heading back out to the set. Mallory met him on the set in a white robe, but she wouldn't meet his eyes.

"Okay, you two. Ready?" the director asked.

He nodded.

"Then get under the sheets. This scene picks up again after you've supposedly made love. Got it?"

Mallory took off her robe and handed it to someone. She was in a low-fitting strapless bra and tight tan boy shorts made from some silky material. The outfit was much less revealing than a string bikini, but the mere thought she'd look naked under the sheets had Roberto's imagination running wild and his fingers itching to touch her skin.

She climbed into the bed and drew the sheets to her chest. Roberto climbed in next to her. A few hoots and catcalls came from the cast and crew at the fringe of the set.

He reached out with his toes and rubbed her calf. Her skin felt as smooth as the finish on his sports car. "This is strange," he whispered.

"Only because it's pretend."

"Well, I, for one," he whispered, "am all for making it real, but not in front of an audience."

Her lips moved into a smile, but no emotion reached her eyes. "This is as close as you're going to get, loverboy."

"What's wrong?"

"Mallory," the director said. "Roberto. We'll be panning the cameras on you from various angles for three minutes. You guys gotta keep the heat up."

That wasn't going to be a problem. Cooling him off would be. Roberto scooted close to her, entangled his legs in hers. He did what felt natural by leaning on his elbow, resting his head in his hand and leaning over her. Her body yielded to him in softness.

"Five, four, three, two and…"

He glanced into her eyes. Something was terribly wrong. "I'm glad you came," he said, trying to sound convincing.

"Me, too."

"You know this…isn't forever," he said.

"Nothing ever is."

"Good." He leaned down and kissed her. Giving them hot was no problem. He closed his eyes and slanted his mouth over hers.

She pushed him away.

Oh, yeah. They had other lines.

"What happens in Charlotte…" she said.

"Stays in Charlotte," he finished, then went back to kissing her. Now the cameras were panning and he didn't care. With Mallory's lips under his, the fact that people stood around the set dissolved from his memory. She was in his arms, their skin touching.

Someone coughed next to the bed, and he felt Mallory go completely still. The director must've called cut and, lost in each other, they hadn't heard him. She whipped off the covers and all but jumped onto the set floor. She snatched up her robe and ran off, presumably toward her dressing room.

Roberto, on the other hand, let his head fall back against the pillow, giving himself a minute to adjust. No one else seemed to be paying a lick of attention to him except for the makeup lady.

With a grin on her face, she held his robe out for him. "That was some acting." She chuckled.

"Thank you." He cinched the belt and stalked off toward Mallory's dressing room. He knocked on the door. "Mallory?"

The door opened and she stood there, already dressed in jeans and a T-shirt.

"Are you okay?"

"I'm fine."

Right. He made a mental note to never suggest she bluff in a poker game, but he knew when to fold. "I have to head back to Charlotte later tonight, but can you go out to dinner with me?"

"Sorry, I've got plans."

"Are you coming to Darlington this weekend?" He braced himself for her answer.

"I can't." She walked away and then, seeming to have second thoughts, turned around. "And it wouldn't be a good idea for you to come to my parents' anniversary party in Dover. I'm sorry." She looked it, too. Theo Stein had obviously gotten to her.

"It's okay."

"I... My hours will be crazy this next month." She swallowed, clearly uncomfortable.

"I get it."

"No," she said. "I'm sure you don't."

He'd given women brush-offs enough times to know one when he heard it. Being on the receiving end wouldn't have felt so terrible, but for the fact that this was Mallory. "Not a big deal," he said, in the hope of making her—and himself—feel better. "I have one more cameo left. I'll see you then." He turned away.

He'd known this would happen. His warning flags had been frantically flapping for weeks now. He reminded himself she was a woman, like all the rest. Fickle, manipulative and untrustworthy. Only he had a feeling that no matter what he did, or didn't do, he was kidding himself. This woman was going to haunt him the rest of his life.

CHAPTER FIFTEEN

MALLORY HAD REJECTED *the* Roberto Castillo.

She hadn't seen him in weeks, and each day passed feeling more gloomy and miserable than the last. While she'd accepted that Theo had probably been right and she was little more than the one who had gotten away as far as Roberto was concerned, her feelings for him were a bit more complicated. Try as she might to sort through them, she couldn't.

As she and Tara drove from the Baltimore airport late Friday afternoon to their parents' fortieth anniversary celebration, she was as confused and conflicted as she had been the last time she'd seen Roberto on the *Racing Hearts* set all those weeks ago. Lying in bed with him, despite being in front of a camera, had been one of the most bittersweet moments in her life. She'd gone to sleep every night since then imagining what it had felt like being held in his arms. As they neared the motor home parking at the Dover track, the possibility of seeing him again, even on TV, was at once terrifying and thrilling.

"Earth to Mallory," Tara said from the driver's seat of their rented compact.

"Sorry," Mallory said, adjusting her sunglasses. "Did you say something?"

"Are you okay?"

"Good. Fine. Just tired. Been working a lot."

"Hey, how did your callback go?"

Standing in front of the casting director, the movie director and a couple of the producers had been the most nerve-racking moment of her life, but then she'd started in on the lines and the character had come to life in her head. "Good," she said. "I think."

"Are they still worried about you being typecast?"

"I'm not sure. I think all that controversy over me being with Roberto in Mexico might've done the trick."

"You couldn't turn on the entertainment news for a week without hearing about it. Are you seeing Roberto this weekend?"

"No." She looked out the window.

"I thought you were going to invite him to Mom and Dad's party."

"Well, our…arrangement kind of ended."

"Whoa."

"I feel bad, though. Mom and Dad will be so disappointed. They were looking forward to meeting him."

"They'll deal. You're more important to them than some driver."

"They'd probably still want me to ask for infield passes for us to go and visit him."

"What about you?" Tara asked. "And what you want?"

"That's the thing. I'm not sure I know what I want."

PATSY AND DEAN HADN'T HEARD about the bedroom scene on *Racing Hearts,* and Roberto did his best to avoid them, pouring himself into his job. Racing always had been, always would be where he belonged. And with each NASCAR race and every lap he racked up, he became more and more comfortable with his team, his car, the tracks.

He'd even broken the ice in Darlington and stayed in the motor home Cargill-Grosso Racing had set up for him in the owners' and drivers' lot. Turned out he'd actually enjoyed kicking back with Kent and his new wife, Tanya, and a few other drivers and their wives. Although without Mallory by his side, he'd felt as if something had been missing.

Knowing she'd be at Dover the entire weekend for the anniversary party had him dreading that race. Roberto was scheduled to race both the NASCAR Nationwide and NASCAR Sprint Cup Series events, so he planned on staying extremely busy. He had, though, found the time to make a few calls to determine where the Daltons were staying, and had, more than once, caught himself wanting to crash their party. For once in his life, the ball was in a woman's court, and the feeling didn't sit well.

He needed a break. Some quiet time to clear his head, and the best place to do that was home, in Argentina. He hadn't seen his father since the hectic racing season had started, so he was looking forward to finishing the Dover race and flying immediately to South America.

After a long but relatively uneventful race, Roberto crossed Dover's finish line in twelfth position. He drove his car to the garage, hopped out and ran through the requisite interviews.

Before he could leave for the airstrip, Dean called out from one of the garage stalls "Roberto? Can we talk to you?"

"In private," Patsy added, waving Roberto to one corner of an end stall.

Dios...they must've seen the last cameo. "Sure." Roberto followed them, getting ready for a chunk to be taken out of his thick hide.

Instead, he was taken aback by a man he'd never met before leaning against the wall. He had light-colored hair and pale blue eyes and seemed unusually alert.

"Roberto, this is my cousin, Jake McMasters," Patsy said.

The private investigator. "Hello." Roberto shook his hand, wondering what this could possibly have to do with him.

"Jake's been doing some research for us," Dean offered. "Relating to the disappearance of our daughter Gina when she was a baby."

"Yeah, I have heard you two talking about it now and again. How's it going?"

"Slowly," Patsy said. "He's looked back on records and re-searched adoptions in several states for the three years surrounding Gina's disappearance."

"How can I help?" Roberto said.

"Well, this is a little touchy," Dean said.

"Surprising, actually," Patsy added.

McMasters set down his coffee cup and rolled forward on the balls of his feet, all business. "How much do you know about the Dalton family?"

Patsy put her hand out, silencing McMasters.

Roberto glanced at Patsy. "What does this have to do with the Daltons?"

"There's no easy way to say this, Patsy," McMasters said.

"I know." She looked toward Roberto, concern in her eyes. "You've been seeing a lot of Mallory these days."

"What does she have to do with this?"

"Well, Jake's research uncovered that Mallory, that is, Mary-Jean Dalton, is actually an adopted child."

"What?" She'd never said anything about being adopted.

"Apparently, the Daltons were having difficulty having children. They adopted Mary-Jean, but the records concerning her birth parents were destroyed in an Iredell County fire more than twenty years ago."

"No one seems to remember much about it. Not even relatives."

"To think she might have been under our noses all this time," Patsy said, her eyes welling with tears. "I stood right next to her. Talked to her at the NASCAR Awards Banquet."

"Is it possible?" Dean asked, looking at Roberto with anticipation in his eyes. "That she's really Gina?"

Roberto had come to respect these two in a very short time. They were as committed to each other as Roberto had ever seen. Theirs was a true partnership, and now the hope, expectation and yearning in their eyes almost hurt, but his first instinct was to protect Mallory.

"Anything is possible," Roberto said. "But I'm going to guess that she doesn't know she's adopted."

"She's never said anything to you about it?"

"No." She would've brought up her own adoption if she were aware of it. "Are you positive you didn't make a mistake?" Roberto looked to McMasters.

"There's no doubt about it. She's adopted."

"Why would they keep something like this from her unless the adoption was suspect?" Dean asked.

"I don't know," Roberto said. "I have not met her parents. But it could be as simple as them not wanting Mallory to know the truth."

"If they have nothing to hide," McMasters said, "then why won't they return my phone calls?"

That, in and of itself, seemed suspect.

"Find them," Dean said to McMasters. "Confront them. I want answers. Now. I want you to talk to them before the FBI gets to them."

"I checked into it," McMasters said. "They're staying here until tomorrow. Here at the track."

"Wait," Roberto said, looking toward Dean and Patsy. "You don't know they have done anything illegal."

"There are an awful lot of pieces that aren't fitting together," Patsy said.

That, Roberto couldn't argue. "They are celebrating their fortieth wedding anniversary this weekend," he said. "And have a lot of guests. Can this wait?"

"We've already waited thirty years," Dean said.

"Don't make us wait one more day," Patsy added.

Trying to think of another option, Roberto let out a long breath. "Can you at least let me talk to them first?"

Dean looked toward Patsy and she nodded. "You have half an hour," Dean said.

As was typical for their race weekends, Mallory's mom and dad had come with a slew of friends and relatives. This time, though, being it was their fortieth anniversary celebration, they'd reserved ten motor home spots. In all, the Dalton crew had nearly an entire section to themselves. They'd parked their motor homes back to back, creating a large, shared gathering area in a center, grassy space.

Tents had been erected to create cool shade over groups of tables and chairs. Grills were aligned on one side, coolers on the other. All weekend, there'd been music and sunshine and Mallory would've been having a wonderful time if she'd never met

Roberto. Instead, the fact that he was a short distance away made it hard for her to concentrate on anything else.

The race had ended, and while the rest of the campground packed up to head home, the entire Dalton crew was staying one last night to avoid the crush, and then they were all heading to an oceanside resort for a few more days of revelry.

Mallory's dad, his arm around Mallory's mom, held a champagne glass high in the air. "Here's to forty more years!"

The group cheered and clinked their glasses left and right. Buddy and Shirley kissed and Mallory raised her own bottle of water. "Mom and Dad, I'm so proud of you two. You've been wonderful role models, and I hope to have a marriage half as wonderful as yours."

"Me, too!" Tara stood. "Congratulations!"

"Hey, Tara!" one of their uncles yelled. "We heard wedding bells will soon be ringing!"

Everyone looked toward Tara, who stood next to Adam Sanford, owner of Sanford Racing. She flashed a gorgeous engagement ring on her left hand. "You heard right." Tara laughed.

"What about you, Mallory?" someone else yelled and all heads spun in her direction.

"Don't anyone hold their breath." Mallory glanced up to see a man, looking strangely suspicious, approaching their tables. For such a warm day, he was overdressed, wearing a sweatshirt with the hood drawn over his head. A baseball cap and sunglasses made it impossible to see his face, but he was making a beeline straight for her.

Mallory narrowed her eyes at him and then his gait triggered recognition. *Roberto. Oh God.* Hoping no one had seen or recognized him, she sped to meet him, took his arm and pulled him off to the side. "What are you doing here?"

"I'm sorry. I know you didn't want me here."

"I'm actually glad you came."

"Mallory, I…" He flipped back his hood. "I need to talk to your parents."

"Well, look who's here," someone yelled.

And for the next several minutes, Mallory stood back while people surrounded Roberto, introducing themselves and welcoming him. When he started looking a bit agitated, Mallory went to his rescue. "Come on." She drew him away from the group. "Since you're here, you might as well meet my mom and dad." She took him to the other side of the camp and stopped by her parents' chairs. "Mom. Dad. Roberto stopped by after all."

They stood, clearly delighted.

"Congratulations, Mr. and Mrs. Dalton." Roberto shook their hands.

"Please call us Shirley and Buddy," her mom said, squeezing his arm.

"You ran a good race today," her dad said.

"Thank you."

"So we've decided," her mom added.

"You're our new driver," her dad said.

Great. Wonderful.

"I'm flattered." Roberto nodded.

Mallory smiled at Roberto. "It may not seem like much, but they've been Dean Grosso fans since the beginning of time. They like you."

"I know this is going to seem awkward." Roberto's smile turned to a frown as he glanced uncertainly at her. "But do you mind if I talk to them in private for a minute?"

Mallory studied him. "No. Go ahead."

"What's going on?" her dad asked.

"Can we go into your motor home?"

"Sure," her mom said, leading the way.

"I'll be back in a minute," Roberto said and followed her parents.

As Mallory watched them climb the steps to her parents' motor home, a sense of dread overwhelmed her.

CHAPTER SIXTEEN

"THANK YOU for coming today, Roberto," Shirley said.

"Unfortunately, I'm not here for social reasons," Roberto said, hating to do this on their anniversary. "And we don't have much time."

"What's going on?" Buddy said.

"A few months ago Dean and Patsy Grosso hired a private detective to find their missing daughter, Gina. I'm sure you have heard about it in the news. How the FBI has reopened the case?"

They both nodded.

"It's terrible," Shirley commented. "How could someone kidnap a baby?"

"Their investigator discovered that Mallory was adopted around the time of Gina's disappearance."

Shirley and Buddy exchanged glances and Buddy put his arm around Shirley's shoulder. "So?" he said, his features turning guarded. "What does that have to do with us?"

"Did you know that Mallory's adoption records were destroyed in a fire?"

"No."

"Then why haven't you returned Jake McMasters's phone calls?"

"We've been a little busy here, with the anniversary party," Buddy said, not a little defensively. "And I don't like what you're implying."

"Look," Roberto said. "McMasters is going to be here any minute now. I couldn't stop him. With you keeping Mallory's adoption secret, he thinks…he thinks Mallory might be Gina Grosso."

"That's ridiculous!" Buddy said.

"Is it?"

Shirley frowned, her gaze turned downcast. "She's not Gina, Roberto."

"Can you prove it?"

She nodded.

"We've got the records in our safe-deposit box," Buddy added.

"But this is going to become public, isn't it?" Shirley asked.

"I don't know if something like this can be kept quiet with Mallory being an actress." Roberto sighed. "The press is all over this search for the missing Gina, and it sounds like the FBI might want to question you, too."

"So what do we do now?"

"You don't have anything to hide, right?"

"No," Buddy said.

"But Mallory doesn't know she's adopted," Shirley added.

"She's going to find out," Roberto said. "I think you need to tell her. Now." He glanced at his watch. "You have ten minutes."

MALLORY WATCHED the motor home windows, wondering what in the world Roberto had to say to her parents. Through the windows, she could see him pacing back and forth in the living room, clearly upset about something.

"Maybe he's old-fashioned," Tara said with a smile. "And he's asking Dad for your hand in marriage."

"Not going to happen." Mallory rolled her eyes.

"Hey, he likes you. A lot. That, if nothing else, is apparent by the fact that he showed up here today."

"Trust me. He's not the marrying kind."

"Mary-Jean?" Her dad stuck his head out of the motor home. "Can we talk to you for a minute?"

"In the motor home," Shirley said, looking as if she were about to walk in front of a firing squad.

Mallory didn't feel much better. "Roberto?" she said, coming beside him. "What's going on?"

"It's okay," he reassured her. "I'll wait outside."

So much for the marriage proposal.

"No." Shirley touched his arm. "Could you stay? For Mallory?"

"I'm not sure she'll want me here." Roberto glanced at her. "This is family business."

"Stay. Please," Mallory said, suddenly panicking. She looked back and forth between her parents. "What in the world is going on?"

"Sit down, honey," her dad said.

"No." She paced into the kitchen area and spun back toward them. "Tell me."

Her mom sighed. "There's something…something we should have told you a long, long time ago."

"But the right time never seemed to come," Buddy added.

"You're scaring me." She came back into the living room and stood next to Roberto. He'd stepped back and out of the way, as if he wanted to disappear.

"You don't need to be frightened. It's just…" said Shirley.

"We don't want you to hear this from somewhere else. It's going to come as a bit of a surprise," Buddy added.

"You know we tried to have children for a long time before you came along."

She nodded.

"Almost ten years of trying."

"Well, we all but gave up and looked into adoption. There was this nice young woman. Unmarried. And pregnant."

"She was the housekeeper for the Ramaleys down the street from us."

"Well, we… There isn't any easy way to say this," said Buddy.

"We adopted you. When you were only three days old." Her mother's face turned dreamy-looking. "I'll never forget bringing you home. We were so happy to finally have a baby."

Mallory couldn't have heard right. The volume control on her ears seemed to be going out. At first her mother's voice sounded loud and then her mouth would move and Mallory could hear nothing. "What are you talking about?" Unconsciously, she reached for Roberto's hand. "You're not making any sense."

"We adopted you," her dad said. "I'm not sure how else to explain it."

"Tara, too? And Emma-Lee?"

"No, dear. I don't know how it happened." Her mother shrugged. "But I got pregnant with Tara before you were a year old. Even Emma-Lee came easy."

"Let me get this straight." This had to be some weird dream. Any minute now she'd wake up. "I'm adopted? But Tara and Emma-Lee aren't?"

Both her parents nodded.

Mallory's world tilted. This wasn't a dream. She was here, in her parents' motor home, breathing, standing next to Roberto.

Adopted.

That meant her aunts and uncles, her grandparents, her parents, her sisters really didn't belong to her. Worse, she didn't belong to them. If not for Roberto putting his arm around her shoulder and holding her steady, she may have fallen down.

"Your…birth mother…wanted a completely closed adoption. She was only seventeen and didn't want her family to know. She said they would've never let her marry the father, some boy from out of town, and wanted it all kept as secret as possible."

"She moved to California right after you were born," added her father.

"And my father?"

"We don't know anything about him," her mother answered.

"We had every intention of telling you when you were old enough to understand."

"But as you got older, you noticed how your dark coloring was different from Tara and Emma-Lee."

"Different from all of us."

"And we could tell it bothered you."

"So you lied," said Mallory.

"No. Well, yes, but it wasn't intentional. It just came out one day. I remember it so clearly. You were in second grade and you and Tara came home with your school pictures. You looked at yours and you looked at hers and you started crying. Cried and cried and cried. You wanted blond hair. Blue eyes. You hated the way you looked," said Shirley.

"I remember that," Mallory whispered. "I remember."

Roberto didn't say anything, only tightened his hold on her.

"You were so upset that we all had blond hair and blue eyes and you didn't. Well, I couldn't stand you crying, so I latched on to the first thing I could think of. I pulled out a picture of my grandma. She had dark hair and brown eyes, like you. She was so pretty. Everyone always said she stood out like a red rose in a sea of white daisies.

"That got you to stop crying in a second. In fact, you grinned. Seemed like you were happy as could be to look like your grandma.

"After that, we didn't know how to tell you the truth. And we heard so many terrible stories of kids who found out they were adopted rebelling against their families and becoming teenage delinquents. We wanted the best for you.

"Mary-Jean, you have to believe that it never mattered to us. Your being adopted didn't seem important."

"To you." She went limp against Roberto. "All my life, I've felt like I didn't belong. Turns out I was right all along."

"Was it us?"

"Did we treat you differently?" asked Buddy.

She thought back. Oh, there were the usual squabbles that every family endured, but she'd never truly felt they'd favored Tara. Emma-Lee possibly a little, but she was the baby. Had she ever truly felt slighted? "No. But still, you should've told me."

"We thought it would make you feel more like you didn't belong."

"Lying wasn't the answer."

"We've made a lot of mistakes, Mary-Jean. Parents always do. Loving you enough wasn't one of them," said her father.

She knew that. Felt it. But just now, that didn't seem to be enough. "Why are you telling me this? Now. Why now?"

"We didn't have a choice."

Roberto explained about the Grossos' search for their kidnapped baby leading them to Mallory's birth records.

"Am I Gina Grosso?"

"No," said Buddy.

"Don't lie to me again. Please," she whispered. "Am I a Grosso?"

"No!" Shirley yelled.

Mallory squeezed Roberto's hand and he rubbed her arm as he continued to hold her. "What was her name then?" she whispered. "My real mother?"

"Luisa Moreno."

Luisa Moreno.

"Was she Latina? I'm Latina?"

"Mexican, I think," her father said. "But I got the sense your father was Caucasian."

Mallory had to get out of this motor home. Away from...these people. She struggled free of Roberto's arms, ran back to the tiny bedroom she was sharing with Emma-Lee and threw her stuff in her bag.

Shirley stood in the hall. "Mallory, wait."

"I have to get out of here." She pushed past the doorway.

"Sweetheart!" Buddy reached out.

"Don't call me sweetheart! Ever again!" Mallory raced out of the motor home.

"Mallory!" Tara stood from one of the tables.

"What's going on?" Emma-Lee asked.

She turned toward her sisters. Mallory didn't belong here. She didn't belong anywhere. "Ask them." She nodded toward the motor home. "Ask your parents." Mallory hiked her bag onto her shoulders and ran down the dirt road.

"Mallory!" The sound of Roberto's voice came from behind her. "Slow down. Please." He caught up with her.

Vaguely, she became aware of the racing fans looking at Roberto as if they couldn't believe he was in the campground area. He shoved on his sunglasses and baseball cap.

"I'm sorry," she said. "You shouldn't have had to go through that."

"Me?" He stopped her and held her face in his hands. "Don't worry about me. Are you okay?"

"I don't know." She hugged herself. "I... This is the strangest feeling. I don't know where I belong. I feel like I don't know anything anymore." She cried. "Who am I?"

"Shh." He drew her into his arms and held her.

"Where do I go?" she said, her voice cracking. "What do I do?"

"Can you get away from work for a few days?"

She nodded. "I had been planning on going to the ocean after the race. With my fam...family."

"You want to get out of here?"

"Sounds tempting."

"Come on." He set his baseball cap low on her head, grabbed her hand and ran toward the track airfield. "It's only a couple days, but it might be all you need to clear your mind."

Warning bells clanged inside her head at the thought of being alone with Roberto. She stopped in her tracks, her heart racing. "I'm not sure this is a good idea. You. Me. Alone."

"We won't be alone. Unless you want to be."

Still, she hesitated.

"No photographers, no press, no fans. Fresh air, peace and quiet."

"That sounds like heaven."

"No," he whispered, drawing her along. "That's Argentina."

CHAPTER SEVENTEEN

FINALLY, she'd fallen asleep.

On his private jet, Roberto sat across from Mallory and studied her tranquil face, marveled at how different she looked at this moment from several hours earlier when she'd been deep in thought, digesting this sudden alteration of her world. Her face had been a mass of furrows and lines, her eyes deeply troubled, but she'd said barely a word. All in all, she'd handled the news of being adopted fairly well, better than he would have, anyway.

He'd coerced her into eating half of a ham sandwich and a cup of tomato basil soup and that'd been the ticket. Something warm in her stomach combined with the steady hum and vibrations of the engine had lulled her to sleep on the couch.

Now, Roberto tried putting himself in her place, imagining how he would feel if his father had told him the exact same thing. He'd be angry and hurt and extremely confused, as he'd been when he'd found out his mother was still alive. And it'd shaken his trust in his father for a time.

But suddenly discovering that his mother was not of Roberto's blood wouldn't bother him. That would likely be more of a relief than anything. But his father? The man who had grounded him to this earth? That would be a different story, a complete betrayal, rocking his world and setting him to questioning everything he'd ever known or believed in.

He reached for a blanket from a nearby cabinet and gently placed it over Mallory's still frame, feeling something he could only label as protectiveness toward her. It was something he was unaccustomed to, as unaccustomed as he was to experiencing feelings of friendship toward a woman. But he felt that, too.

He had to be crazy, bringing her with him to Argentina. Patsy Grosso was going to disown him. At the time he'd made the suggestion, it'd felt like the right thing to do for a friend. She'd desperately needed to get away, to think, and his home outside Buenos Aires was quiet, peaceful. There would be no one to bother her, no family, no press. No one. She'd be free to do as she pleased with no demands on her time or her thoughts. This might prove to be the best thing for Mallory, but, for Roberto, this was the making of a disaster.

He'd brought women home before, plenty of them; that wasn't the issue. But he'd brought them, knowing full well that they wouldn't like the country setting and the simple people, knowing they'd be antsy to leave, usually sooner rather than later, claiming they were too far from the city, the restaurants, the shopping, the nightlife. He'd brought the women never caring what any of them might think of his *estancia* or his father. In fact, he'd always been secretly pleased when they couldn't stand the place, preferring his apartment in the heart of Buenos Aires, when they thought his father coarse and unsophisticated. He supposed it had been one more way he'd distanced himself from all the women he'd dated and proved they were all wrong for him.

This time, though, was different. No matter what he tried to tell himself, he cared what Mallory might think of his favorite home. This woman who'd blown him off a few short weeks ago. This woman he wanted with an ache threatening to consume him. More frightening than that, he was beginning to think he might actually care for her. She was different from the rest in so many ways.

He tucked the blanket around her, letting his hand linger on her back, and then he lay down on the couch across from her and gazed at her face. Getting this woman into bed wasn't going to get her out of his head.

And you are taking this woman to Argentina with you. You are insane, amigo. Completely insane.

"MALLORY." Roberto's quiet voice along with the touch of a hand gently rubbing her arm penetrated her senses. "Wake up, *querida*."

Feeling groggy and fuzzy-headed, she sat and ran her hands through her tangled hair. "Where am I?"

"About to land in Argentina. Let's get you buckled up." He lifted her into a forward-facing seat, connected her belt and tightened the strap. Then he sat next to her. "Feeling better?"

"I'm not sure." She yawned and glanced out the window. It looked to be late morning. "What day is it? I've lost all track of time."

"Monday. We flew through the night while you slept."

"Did you sleep, too?"

He nodded. "Most of the way."

They landed on a small airstrip in the countryside. The pilot taxied across the runway to a hangar and then Roberto unlatched the main door. "Are you awake enough to make it down the steps on your own?"

His attentiveness surprised but warmed her. "I'm good."

"Thank you," he said to his pilot. "We won't need you again until early Thursday morning."

She was here for three days. And three nights. Theo's warning came out of nowhere. *Once you make love with him, you become another conquest. One more name tacked on to a long list of women.*

She couldn't think about that. Not now. His offer for her to accompany him here had been sincere. She refused to believe anything different. Theo was wrong. He had to be.

The pilot nodded. "Let me know what time and I'll be here."

Mallory followed Roberto outside and into the warmth and sunlight. Fluffy white clouds dotted a brilliant blue sky, but the air carried a slight chill. "I expected it to be hot."

"This is Argentina's autumn. It'll be winter soon." He threw their bags in the back of a golf cart and they took the cart down a path across a field. After a few moments, Roberto stopped at the edge of a hill and watched her reaction. "This is it. Welcome to my home."

This place seemed special to Roberto, and when she glanced

up, she understood why. A scene, as picturesque as a tourist postcard, was spread out before her. They were parked overlooking a grove of tall trees surrounding a large country home with a stone foundation, a sweeping front porch and backyard filled with trees turning color with the change of season. The vineyard, too, looked blanketed in the oranges, reds, browns and yellows of autumn.

"It's beautiful. Where are we?"

"An hour or so northwest of Buenos Aires. Near a town called San Antonio de Areco. The birthplace of the *gaucho.* That's the main house over there, and there are several guesthouses." He gestured toward the largest building and then toward several smaller adobe cottages. They all shared a large swimming pool.

"You have horses." Mallory pointed to a barn, paddock and the large fenced-in area some distance from the main house.

"My *father* has horses. Sheep and goats, too. You can take the *gaucho* off the farm, but not the farm out of the *gaucho.* The animals keep him happy."

"And a vineyard." Rows and rows of plants covered what looked like several hundred acres of land in the distance.

"*Sí.* The animals are for fun, but he works the vineyard, harvests the grapes, makes wine. Too bad. We missed the grape harvest by a few months."

They took the cart down the hill and parked near the front door. As soon as they stepped inside the house, Mallory smelled something wonderful cooking—meat and onions and spices— and realized she was starving. She hadn't eaten anything since yesterday afternoon.

Roberto set their bags in the foyer and walked her from room to room. This house was as light and airy as his Mexico City home was luxurious and rich. Mexico City, and quite likely the rest of his city dwellings, were little more than hotels. This was a home. The walls were a creamy-colored stucco that contrasted beautifully with the dark woodwork. Colorful wool rugs covered the rustic wood floors, and sturdy, functional furniture filled every room.

"It's so quiet," she whispered. "Is your father the only one who lives here?"

"*Dios,* no. Most of the time this place is like a little village. Several workers and their families live in the guest homes on the property."

"Then where is everyone?"

"Working. Probably outside. This is a busy time of year. Getting ready for winter."

They walked into the kitchen and a stout middle-aged woman, her black hair piled on top of her head, spun around from a large stove. "Roberto!" A stream of Spanish Mallory couldn't hope to understand spilled excitedly from the woman's mouth as she hugged him. "You are late!"

When she finally took a breath, Roberto turned. *"Emilia, ésta es Mallory."*

Mallory shook her hand. *"Hola."*

"Hola, Mallory. I'm so happy to meet you," she said in heavily accented English.

"I know you weren't expecting me," Mallory said. "I hope I'm no trouble."

Emilia waved her concerns away. "The more, the merrier."

"Can she stay in one of the guest bedrooms?"

"Of course, Roberto. It's almost time for lunch. Are you two hungry?"

"Starving." Roberto smiled. "Mallory, sit down and relax. I'll take care of our bags and be back in a few minutes." He disappeared the way they'd come.

"Something to drink?" Emilia asked.

"That'd be nice, if you don't mind."

While Emilia prepared a hot drink of dried herbs and hot water in a cup curiously shaped like a gourd, Mallory glanced around. The kitchen was spacious, with a long, heavy table meant for seating large groups. A back door opened to what looked like a patio or veranda.

"Here you are." Emilia dropped a metal straw into the cup and handed it to Mallory.

"What is this?"

"*Mate.* Like tea."

Chunks of dried and crushed leaves floated in the liquid. Mallory took a sip, expecting to get a mouthful of herbs. Though the taste was strong and pungent, the *mate* was only a little grainy. She lifted the metal straw to find its end flared with small holes filtering the liquid.

"Can I help with anything?" Mallory asked.

"No. *En absoluto.*" She pushed Mallory toward the door. "Now go. Sit outside and relax. We'll eat soon."

Mallory wandered out back through a set of French doors. She stepped down onto the shaded lawn. A man wearing a wide-brimmed hat, khaki pants and a dark green shirt stood on a ladder, a set of clippers in his hands, trimming a vine climbing the side of the house. He was lean and handsome with only a graying goatee to give away that he was past middle age.

"*Hola,*" she said.

He glanced down and smiled. "*Buenos días, señorita.*"

"Is that a rose vine?"

"*Sí.*"

The plant was loaded with red blossoms. "It's beautiful."

"*Gracias.* I do much of the gardening."

"You have a very green thumb." She glanced around the expansive yard. Many of the plant varieties looked unfamiliar, but the trees in the distance looked to be of some kind of fruit. She pointed to another set of trees closer to the house. "Are those olive trees?"

"*Sí.* We also have plum, pear, fig, peach, quince, apricot and pomegranate."

She laughed. "I thought this was a vineyard, not an orchard."

"We have grapes, too." He nodded. "And nuts. Pecan, walnut, almond."

"If you're trying to impress me, it's working."

"*Bueno.*" He grinned, clipping off a rose and tossing it to her. "It's not as delightful as you, but it's the best I can do on such short notice."

Mallory heard a door shut and footsteps on the patio stones

behind her. Roberto walked toward her and glanced at the rose bud in her hand. He arched one eyebrow. "I see you have met my father."

"I should've known."

Roberto's expression turned quizzical.

"He's a flirt," she explained. "Like you."

Both men laughed.

"I taught him everything he knows." Roberto's father climbed down from his ladder and hugged his son. "It's good to have you home again. How long can you stay?"

"Only a few days."

"It never seems to be enough, but we take what we can get, eh?"

"Mallory, this is Luis. *Papá,* this is my friend Mallory Dalton."

At the word *friend,* Luis's expression turned oddly guarded. "Mallory." When he looked at her, Mallory couldn't help but feel like one in a long line of women *friends* Roberto had brought home over the years. Luis obviously disapproved, and she couldn't blame him. If only she could explain to him that in this case friends really meant just friends. "It's good to meet you, Luis."

He bowed his head. "If there's anything you need while you are visiting, let me know."

"Thank you."

"Come, Mallory," Roberto said. "I'll show you to your room."

She felt Luis's eyes on her as she followed Roberto back into the house and down a hall.

Roberto opened a wooden door, carved with an intricate geometric pattern, and stepped back. "Will this work?"

The moment she walked through the doorway, her entire body relaxed in expectation of sleeping in that inviting and gorgeous bed. The focal point of the room, the large, four-poster had a massive headboard of dark, ornately carved wood. An old-fashioned white coverlet trimmed in colorfully embroidered flowers lay atop a fluffy comforter, and the design repeated on the pillows piled at the head of the bed.

Her suitcase had been laid out for her on top of an antique wooden chest at the foot of the bed. The wood-plank floor was covered with a large wool rug colored in a geometric pattern in reds, browns and creams. French doors opened out to the patio that ran along the length of the back of the house.

"It's beautiful. Perfect."

"There's a TV here." He opened the door to an ornately carved wardrobe. "We have satellite, so you can get updated with news and whatnot if you'd like."

"I think, instead, I'll curl up in that bed and sleep for three days."

"If that's what you want," he whispered. "It's okay, you know."

"Thank you." She turned, took a step toward him and kissed him on the cheek. "This is exactly what I needed."

He gripped her arms and held her for a moment. "Mallory, I…" Abruptly, he let her go. "My room is at the end of the hall if you need anything."

LUNCH WAS CASUAL with three places set for Luis, Roberto and Mallory out on the patio. Luis poured her a glass of wine and handed it across the table. *"Salud."* He raised his own glass and drank. "Taste and tell me what you think. It's from our own winery."

"I'm not much of a connoisseur." She took a sip.

"No matter."

"What kind is it?" The wine was full of so many different flavors.

"A malbec. Complex, *sí?*"

She nodded. "And intense."

"What do you first taste?" He leaned his elbows on the table and watched her reaction.

"Um." She glanced at Roberto, but he only smiled and arched his brows.

"Take another sip," Luis commanded.

She did, glancing again at Roberto.

"You are on your own here," he said, grinning. "*Papá* wouldn't talk to me for a week if I coached you."

She turned back to Luis. "I don't know."

"Take an *olor*…a…smell," he said. He showed her what he meant by swirling the wine in his glass and bringing it to his nose.

She followed his example and took a whiff. "Berries?"

"Yes! Now. Taste again."

She let the wine sit on her tongue, feeling amateurish, and then swallowed. "It has a…an oaky flavor?"

"Two for two. Next?"

"I'm not sure." She took another sip. "Maybe…pomegranate?"

Luis threw back his head and howled with laughter.

"I can't believe it!" Roberto chuckled. "You are the first person to guess that one. You have won my father's heart."

"Forever, Mallory," Luis said.

Emilia brought out a casserole dish with steam escaping the porcelain cover. She dished a scoopful into Mallory's flat and wide bowl. "*Gracias,* Emilia," Mallory said. "But I'm not sure I can eat all this."

"Lunch is the main meal in Argentina," Roberto explained. "So…"

"When in Rome…" she added with a smile.

"*Gracias,* Emilia," Luis said, patting the woman's hand.

And then he went on to explain that the main dish was called *estofado,* or stew made with beef shortribs, carrots and onions, and slow cooked until the meat fell right off the bone and practically melted in Mallory's mouth. The accompanying sauce was thick and rich and, rather than the potatoes that would've been served with the stew back in the States, Emilia served steamy fettuccini. "We have many European influences in our country other than Spanish," Luis explained. "Roberto's mother is half-Italian."

"But *Papá* won't be bringing out the baby pictures, *verdad?*"

"No, no. Never again. I learned my lesson after the first time." Luis winked at her. "Roberto's had many *friends* come to visit. Funny, they never come back."

"*Papá.* Stop."

Mallory put her hand on Roberto's arm. "It's okay."

"What?" Luis threw his hands wide. "It's true, isn't it?"

"Roberto and I really are…just friends."

"They say there's a first time for everything, Mallory." Luis studied her for a quiet moment. "For everything."

CHAPTER EIGHTEEN

AFTER LUNCH, Roberto had some business to attend to, so Mallory returned to the guest bedroom and unpacked. More than once, she glanced over at the TV. Finally, she gave in, switched it on and found an English-speaking entertainment channel.

Her worst suspicions were confirmed when, after the announcer finished a segment on the newest pregnant Hollywood couple, the spotlight turned to the latest in the Gina Grosso kidnapping case.

"Could America's Sweetheart actually be none other than the missing Gina Grosso? Though Mallory Dalton's parents refused to comment, news of her secretive adoption obviously hit a chord. While Mallory is nowhere to be found, fans say Roberto Castillo left with an unidentified female on his private jet after last Sunday's race. Word is they flew out of the country. Could it be the two are holed up at his very private rural estate in Argentina? Nervous breakdown or romantic getaway? Either way, looks like Kacy Haughton is finally out of the pict—"

Mallory punched the power button on the remote. Turning that damned thing on had been a mistake. Wanting to clear her head, she left her room and went in search of someone, anyone, who might help her get her mind off that ridiculous news show.

The entire house was deserted. No Roberto, or Luis, or Emilia. She wandered outside, wanting to familiarize herself with the grounds. Within a very short time, she soon discovered that Roberto hadn't been kidding when he'd said she'd find peace and quiet here. There was nothing for a guest to do except relax.

Finally, she made her way toward the backyard and into what

looked like part of the vineyard. There were no grapes on the vines, and the foliage was a striking combination of oranges and yellows. Many of the leaves had already dried and had fallen off the vine. When she spotted Luis on a tractor heading toward her down one of the rows, she waved. When he got closer, he nodded, shut off the motor and hopped down. *"Buenas tardes,"* he said.

"Hola."

"You didn't rest?"

"If I do I won't sleep tonight."

But he'd noticed her momentary hesitation. "Too noisy? Too hot or cold? Hungry? Overtired?"

"A lot on my mind. I'll be all right." She walked around the tractor, hoping to change the subject. "Do you know where Roberto is?"

"In the garage working on one of the trucks."

"What are you doing?"

"Weeding and tilling the soil a bit." He pointed to a piece of equipment he was towing behind the tractor. "That contraption gets in close to the vines."

"Do you make your wine here?"

"Sí. We have a winery this way. Come. I'll give you a quick tour." He walked toward the other side of the house. "They may be bottling some of the young wines today."

"I'd love to see it." She followed by his side.

"How long have you known Roberto?" he asked.

"Only a few months."

"Ah," Luis said with a smile. "But it's you I have seen on TV on the war wagon, *sí?"*

She nodded. "I've been to a few races. Do you ever go to the tracks?"

He stopped and flipped his hat back, studying her. "That's very interesting."

"What?"

"In only a few hours, you manage to confront the biggest issue between my son and I."

"I'm sorry. I didn't know—"

"No, no, no. It's all right. After all these years, I have resigned myself to the situation, but I'm not sure Roberto has." He continued on to the winery.

"Resigned yourself to what?" Mallory had to walk fast to keep up.

"He doesn't want me at his races."

"That can't be true."

"What other explanation is there? In more than ten years, he's never invited me. Not once. Now his mother, on the other hand, gets tickets from him for everything."

"You've never been to one of his races here in Argentina?"

"No. Never."

"Ever asked him for tickets?"

He shook his head. "He deals with enough pressure as it is. If he wanted me at the tracks, he'd ask."

They reached the winery and Luis quickly changed the conversation to grapes and processing and bottling, dismissing the topic. Mallory, though, couldn't let it go. Maybe this was one small way she could begin to pay Roberto back for all he'd done for her.

LATER THAT NIGHT, after a light dinner, Mallory helped Emilia clean up and then, exhausted, she'd gone straight to bed. After a sleep broken with bad dreams about her parents, Tara and Emma-Lee, she awoke late the next morning and wandered out to find the kitchen empty. She treated herself to a breakfast of coffee and *dulce de leche* she'd found in the refrigerator and then went back to the guest bedroom for a shower. After drying off, she slathered on some lotion and caught her reflection in the steamy mirror.

It was as if she were seeing herself for the first time. Now that she knew she'd been adopted, she could see it as clearly as the nose on her face. She looked nothing like Shirley and Buddy. Not her heart-shaped face and high cheekbones, not the color of her hair, not her full lips.

As a child, she'd been so desperate to fit in with her family that she'd talked herself into thinking she looked like them. The slant of her nose, she'd tell herself, was similar to Buddy's. The shape of her eyes, if she turned her head a little to the left, reminded her of Shirley. The woman she'd called Mother for thirty years.

Luisa Moreno. What did she look like?

Mallory studied her skin and eyes. She was Latina for sure. Half-Latina, at least. How could she have missed it? All these years. She felt like an idiot.

No. Someone should've told her. Her parents were the idiots. It had been wrong to keep her adoption a secret.

But, then, they were idiots who loved her. That, Mallory could never question. They didn't tell her the truth not because they wanted to hurt her, but because they loved her so much. She didn't doubt that for a moment. They thought they were doing what was right. They'd wanted to make her happy. They didn't understand that knowing why she looked different might've freed her.

"Mallory Moreno." She said it aloud a few times, attempting to roll the *R*'s like Roberto. No, Mallory Dalton still felt right. Better than right. Maybe this wasn't going to be so bad to get used to. She'd already shed the Mary-Jean name, as if a part of her had known it wasn't right for her.

She smiled, suddenly feeling, strangely enough, rather…free. She didn't have to try to fit in anymore, or be anyone. She could be herself. Completely. She could make her own way, independent of her adoptive family.

Someday, very soon, she had a feeling she'd be comfortable in her own light brown skin. She ran her hands through her thick, wavy hair. Suddenly being a brunette felt right. It didn't matter she wasn't blond haired and blue eyed like the rest of the Dalton clan. She looked good in brown. In fact, she looked perfect in brown.

Mallory snatched up her cell phone for the first time since she'd left Dover and her parents' party and listened to the innumerable messages, mostly from her mom, dad and sisters.

The last message was from the director of *Three Sisters*… They were giving Mallory the part for which she'd auditioned. Filming began in less than one month. Mallory squealed to herself. This was good. Things were coming together.

She shook her head, dialed a number and walked toward the window to wait for the international call to connect. She saw Luis was working in the yard, picking the few remaining late-to-harvest apples from one of the trees, when a woman answered the call.

"Hello?" Her voice sounded strained.

What should Mallory call her? *Oh, hell. Get over it*. How could she hold a grudge against someone for doing something from the heart? "Mom?"

"Oh my God. Mary-Jean. Buddy, it's Mary-Jean on the phone."

"It's Mallory, Mother. Mallory."

"What?"

"Say it. I want you to say it. M-a-l-l-o-r-y." Damn, that felt good, putting her foot down with them.

There was a slight pause. "You're right, dear. It's Mallory, not Mary-Jean. I can't promise I'll never forget again, but I'll try."

One stubborn parent down, one to go. Absently, she watched Luis get down from his ladder, position it so he could reach another section of the tree and continue working. The phone clicked as her dad got on another line. "Dad, repeat after me. Mallory."

He chuckled. "I'm glad to hear your voice. *Mallory*. We were worried sick about you. There's rumors flying around that you're in Argentina. Is that true?"

"Yes."

"Oh my," her mother said.

"With Roberto?" her father asked.

"Yes. He has a house a few hours from Buenos Aires. His dad lives here, too." Luis put several apples he'd picked into a basket on the ground.

"So you met his father?" her mom asked.

"That means this is getting serious, huh?" her dad added.

"To be honest, I don't know."

"When can we see you again?" asked her dad.

"I'm not sure. I'll be back in a couple days."

"It's Emma-Lee's birthday this coming weekend," her mom said. "We've got infield camping spots reserved. Join us?"

"I'll think about it." For the first time ever, Mallory Dalton felt herself settling into a cozy and comfortable place in the world.

"I guess that's all we can ask for."

Luis got down from the ladder, stretched and noticed her in the window. He grinned and beckoned for her to come outside. As she signaled back that she'd be out in a minute, a thought occurred to her. "On second thought, I'll come to the Pocono race," she said to her parents.

"That's great."

"But I need you to do me a favor."

FROM HIS DESK in the library, Roberto gazed outside across the courtyard and watched Mallory by the paddock near the main barn. Since he'd needed to make a few phone calls and answer some e-mails, she'd decided to get some sunshine and fresh air. She was now leaning against a railing, smoothing the coat of one of his father's horses and talking to the *gauchos*.

Footsteps sounded in the hall, and a moment later his father came into the room. He set a stack of papers on the desk. "There are a few things you need to handle while you're here."

"I'll get to it before I leave."

They both spoke in Spanish. Although Roberto was as comfortable with English these days, Spanish was his father's preferred means of communication.

Following Roberto's gaze, Luis looked out the window. "So, it's true what she said? She's not like your other women friends?"

"*Sí*, it's true."

"Then why did you bring her here? Is she in trouble?"

"No, *Papá*. She needed some time away."

"And she thinks she's safe coming here with you? Isn't that a little like the deer running straight into the jaguar's den?"

"That's not fair."

"Isn't it?"

"No!" Roberto turned on him, suddenly angry. He'd been thinking about this for a long time, and for a long time it'd been bothering him. "Why did you tell me my mother died when I was born?"

"What does that have to do with this?"

"Everything."

His father studied him. "I told you what I thought you needed to know."

"You always led me to believe that my mother was sweet and loving. That you'd fallen in love with her the first time you met her. And that she'd fallen in love with you."

"So?"

"*Papá,* you didn't bend the truth," Roberto said, frustrated. "You outright lied to me."

"So what if I did? That's the way I wanted to see her in my mind. The way I wanted to remember her."

"The way I thought she was." Roberto stood and walked to the window. "When I ran away to Buenos Aires to find her, I was completely unprepared for the real Camila Franco. Her rejection devastated me." And afterward he'd spent years vying for her attention. He'd even sunk himself into her world and a playboy lifestyle hoping for her eventual acceptance. "It took me a long time to realize that she wasn't the woman you'd led me to believe she could be."

"Would the truth, from the very beginning, have made any difference in your life?"

"I don't know. What is the truth?"

"It's nothing all that extraordinary, I'm afraid." Luis sighed. "I was simply a father wanting, above all else, to protect his son."

"Tell me. All of it."

"All right." Luis sat down, looked out the window and seemed to be gathering his thoughts. "I may have been older than your mother, but I was naive. She seduced me after an argument with her father. I thought we were in love. I thought we would get married. Until she never returned a single one of my letters.

"So I traveled to the city and found her very pregnant and very angry. She wanted an abortion, but her father wouldn't allow it. He kept her locked in the house, so no one would become aware of her condition, and he'd arranged for one of his servant's relatives to take you for a large fee with the promise of secrecy."

"Then how did you manage to get me?"

"She tried every trick in her book to convince me to get her an abortion. I wouldn't do it. When I promised, if she gave you to me, she would never see either one of us again, she only laughed, insisting I would use a baby to get money from her family." Agitated, he paused and ran a hand over his face.

"Finally, after warning her that I'd hound her for the rest of her days if she gave you away to someone else, she handed you to me in the middle of the night. You were so little. Only a day old." His eyes pooled with the memory. "I took you, left Buenos Aires and never once looked back."

"Why tell me she'd died?"

"Simple. I didn't want that woman in your life." He held out his hands as if it should be obvious. "She would have made you question your belief in yourself." His father stood and walked to the window. "I won't apologize, Roberto. The truth about Camila would have hurt you. Held you back. You may never have hoped for something better than life as a *gaucho*."

Roberto tried to imagine if the details of how he'd been conceived, if the kind of person his mother really was would have changed things for him.

"If I had told you your mother didn't want you—or me—you may have grown up thinking there was something wrong with us. That you and I were somehow undeserving of her love. And that, Roberto, is the lie. Look what happened when you found out she was alive."

Roberto nodded. "I get it."

"I know how you yearn, son. You think there is nothing in the world like a mother's love. Trust me, I was angry you couldn't have it. You deserved it, such a beautiful little boy, such a strong and determined young man. My hope was that I could give you enough love for both a mother and a father."

"You did, *Papá*. You always did."

"Good. Because Camila will never be the mother you deserve. But it's not because of who you are, Roberto. It's because of who she isn't. And I'll tell you something else." His father looked out the window and pointed at Mallory. "A woman's love? When you have *that* wholly and completely, you'll discover that a mother's love only goes so far."

"How would you know?" Roberto laughed. "I have never seen you with a woman."

"That doesn't mean it never happened." He grinned. "Your mother might have been the first, but she was not the last woman to break my heart."

"How could you trust again after Camila?"

"I found a woman with so much love bursting from her, she broke the wall around my heart. She died many years ago."

"I'm sorry, *Papá*."

"Don't be." He grinned. "Emilia is doing her own damage these days. But what about your Mallory?"

Roberto looked away. "My arrangement with her is business."

"For you, maybe. Not for her." His father sighed. "Don't break her heart, *el hijo*. She is not your mother."

CHAPTER NINETEEN

BY TUESDAY NIGHT, the ebb and flow of this working ranch had helped Mallory downshift from a stress standpoint into neutral. She was sitting on the veranda with Roberto and his father, drinking a glass of wine when her body slipped into an all-consuming state of lethargy.

Even Roberto seemed to notice. He patted her arm. "Are you all right?"

"Fine," she said. "Just tired. I think I'll call it a night." She stood, thinking it would be best to head back to her bedroom while she could still walk. *"Buenas noches,"* she said.

Roberto quickly came to her side. "You look like you could use some help."

"I'm fine."

"Véte. Ayúdale," Luis said, standing. "Go. Help her. I think Emilia mentioned needing some help with a clogged drain." He winked at Roberto.

Roberto stayed close by her side on the way through the house. When they reached her door, she fought the urge to draw him with her inside the room. "I'll be fine. Really."

He stepped back from her as if touching her would burn. "All right, then. *Buenas noches, querida.*"

"I forgot to tell you." She touched his arm. "I got the *Three Sisters* part."

"Good." He smiled, but his expression seemed sad. "I guess that means you don't need me anymore." He went into his own room, closing the door firmly behind him as she stood watching him from the hall.

Feeling oddly disappointed, Mallory got ready for bed, but when her head hit the pillow, she tossed and turned. Maybe she didn't need Roberto anymore, but she sure as hell wanted him. After a while, she kicked back the covers and snuck out into the hall.

The door to his bedroom was still firmly closed and for a moment she entertained the notion of slipping into his room, climbing in bed with him and dealing with this crazy attraction she felt for him.

Maybe Theo had a point. Only maybe she was the one who needed some romping around under the sheets to put Roberto in place.

Yeah, right. Like that would ever happen.

Swallowing the false bravado, she resolutely turned and headed down to the kitchen. After finding herbal tea in a cupboard, she heated some water in the microwave and then went outside onto the veranda.

She plopped down on the steps and looked into the midnight sky, trying to clear her head. The air was still, but chilly. She held the teacup close to her chest, absorbing its warmth as crickets chirped loudly in every direction. The door opened behind her and Mallory looked back to find Roberto joining her with a blanket in his hand. "You've got to be freezing out here," he said.

"It's colder than I expected."

He spread a wonderfully heavy blanket over her shoulders.

"That feels nice." She tucked it tightly around her.

"Alpaca. Nothing warmer." In flannel pants and a black T-shirt, he sat down next to her. "Couldn't sleep?"

"No. How 'bout you?"

"I was on my laptop going through some e-mails. Heard you moving around."

Neither talked for several minutes.

"I've never seen so many stars," Mallory said, putting her face toward the sky. There were so many twinkling lights that they nearly formed a haze.

"There's only one big city in this country and it's a long distance from here."

"You like coming here, don't you?"

"*Sí.*"

"Why did you ask me to come along?"

"You were in pain. I thought I could help."

"Is that the only reason?"

"I'm at a loss." He glanced into her eyes. "What do you want me to say?"

"Sometimes I feel like the only woman in the world Roberto Castillo has no interest in making love to." She blurted the words out before sense and reason could stop her.

His eyes narrowed. "You think I don't want you? Is that what I heard?"

She nodded. "Yeah. I guess that's it."

He looked away and chuckled, soft and low. "Damned if I do and damned if I don't."

"I don't understand."

"I know." In one swift movement, he laid her gently back on the floor of the veranda. She was in his arms as he was leaning over her, the intensity in his eyes unnerving. Breathless, speechless, Mallory waited. "Pay very close attention, *querida.*"

Slowly, deliberately, he bent toward her, never taking his eyes off hers. When the first gentle touch of his lips came, her eyes drifted closed. As his kiss deepened, turning urgent and feverish, she was lost in sensation. His mouth on hers. His hands on her body. His weight heavy and warm. His leg between her thighs.

Then he drew away, breathing fast. "That…is what it feels like when a man wants a woman."

She pulled him back to her, but he resisted. "Then why…?"

"Before that cameo scene where I kiss you, I hadn't touched a woman, let alone had sex, in more than a year."

"But the media—"

"Lie. All the time," he whispered. "The truth is I had grown very weary of my life. The truth is I'm not sure I wanted all those parties, all those women as much as I fell into a pattern." He trailed his fingertips down her cheek, her neck. "The truth is, *querida,* you make me want in a way I never wanted before." He sat back up, drawing her with him and wrapping the blanket tightly around her. "Satisfied?" Then he stood and walked back into the house, leaving her to stare after him in total confusion.

No, she wasn't satisfied. At all.

THE NEXT MORNING, a day unusually hot and dry for this time of year, Roberto helped his father repair a fence. They were finishing replacing the last post when Mallory came from the house with a pitcher of juice on ice and several cups.

"Thirsty?" she asked.

His father stood. "You are an angel."

"Not me. Emilia. She asked me to bring this out to you two. You can thank her later."

"Maybe I'll thank her now." Luis poured himself a glass and walked toward the house, a shovel resting on his shoulder.

Roberto wiped the sweat from his brow, yanked off his gloves and tossed them on the dusty ground while she poured them both an icy glass of fruit juice.

"What is this?" she asked.

He took a sip. "*Licuados*. A mixture of different juices. Do you like it?"

"I haven't tasted anything yet in this country that I haven't liked." She leaned against a post and took a long gulp. "I've enjoyed my stay. Thanks for bringing me here."

In hindsight, he wouldn't have had it any other way. He liked being with her, whether they slept together or not. "Ready to go home tomorrow?"

"No." She looked away. "*I* may feel differently, but I'm guessing nothing has changed back in the States."

"What did you expect?"

"I don't know. But not what I saw when I turned on the TV the other day. I didn't tell you this, but they're not only speculating that I came to Argentina, but that I've had a nervous breakdown. Can you believe it?"

"Not the kind of press you'd hoped for."

"No."

"Maybe you shouldn't have come here with me."

She studied him. "Do you regret inviting me?"

"Not for a moment." He grabbed a towel and wiped the sweat off his neck. Then a thought occurred to him, something that might go a long way in setting things right. "Mallory, will you do something for me? Will you cut my hair?"

"What? Where did that come from?"

"You have been wanting to get your hands on my head since the first day we met." For some strange reason, he wanted to show the world she had, indeed, made her mark on him. "Now's your chance."

Her eyes widened. "Seriously?"

"Un momento."

"I knew it!" Grinning, she pointed at him. "I knew you wouldn't let me."

"Do you know how to cut hair?"

"I did it for a while after high school."

"Are you any good at it?"

She nodded. "It's like riding a bike. You never forget."

He laughed. "How short?"

"Don't worry about it. You'll look sexier than ever. I swear."

"Let me clean up." He grinned. "Then you can have your way with me."

Ten minutes later, he'd finished with a shower and found Mallory outside. She had a chair and towel set up and had collected scissors and combs from Luis. "All set," she said, the minute he stepped through the door.

"I can see that."

"Sit."

He hoped he wouldn't regret this. The moment he sat in her chair, feeling her presence behind him, knowing she'd be reaching for his head, made him unaccountably nervous.

"Why are you so tense?" Her hands settled on his shoulders and she kneaded his muscles. "Must have been all that work on the fence."

He took a deep breath and forced himself to relax. Her thumbs worked out some knots and he let his head fall forward as she massaged his neck. He didn't even jump when she inched farther and farther up his scalp.

Her fingers were strong and seemed to know their way around tired muscles. Instead of feeling invaded, she made him feel pampered. For the first time, he would hold himself in front of a woman, open and bared, and let her in.

She might break his heart. He could feel the possibility pressing on him, yet he refused to run away. Refused to push her away. Maybe she would love him back, maybe she wouldn't. One way or another, he was going to find out.

He let her grab chunks of his hair and snip them with her scissors. Quietly, his long hair fell in clumps onto the ground, and he closed his eyes. He concentrated on how she touched him, her fingers on his forehead, cool and soft. Her hands in his hair, gentle and loving. She trimmed his hairline, front, back and sideburns, then feathered and layered. Several times she blew cuttings off his cheeks and ears.

Instead of freaking him out, she was turning him on. He imagined her hands moving lower, over his chest, lower still... Just when he was picturing her climbing over him, she whipped the towel off him and declared, "There! Finished!"

She held a mirror out for him to see his reflection. "Well, what do you think?"

The man staring back at him had a distinct similarity to the young boy he'd been. His hair was several inches shorter, but still held a definite curl. "I haven't looked this clean-cut since junior high."

"I think you look incredibly handsome." Her smile turned to a frown. "But, I have to admit, I already miss your hair."

"Too bad. It's gone."

"Why did you let me do that?"

"Why not?"

"When I asked your father for the clippers, he said you've always hated haircuts. Why now? Why me?"

He shrugged. *"No sé."*

"You know I won't hurt you."

"Won't you?"

She cupped her hands on either side of his head. "Never. I promise."

He only wished he could believe and could promise the same. "Okay, that does it," he said.

"Does what?"

He grabbed her hand and pulled her along with him. "Time to let off a little steam."

CHAPTER TWENTY

"A MOTORCYCLE?" Mallory glanced skeptically inside the garage.

"Hey, I'm a Molloy Cycle driver. What would you expect?" He stuffed a small pack into a travel bag strapped to the back of the bike, tossed her a helmet and then grabbed another one for himself.

"I've never been on a motorcycle before."

"Never?"

She shook her head.

"*Dios,* but you have led a sheltered life, Mallory Dalton."

Too sheltered. Mary-Jean kind of sheltered. "Did you know Mallory's not my real name?"

"I thought I heard your parents call you Mary-Jean back in Dover." He studied her thoughtfully. "You look like a Mary-Jean about as much as I look like a Bob."

"The problem is that I don't look like a Dalton, either."

He touched her cheek. "That doesn't change who you are."

"It does. Somehow it does."

He climbed onto his bike. "Hop on, *querida.* Let's go."

At first, Mallory was a bit unnerved moving down the road in the open air, but once she put her arms around Roberto's waist, she felt vibrantly alive. He handled the machine, surely and confidently, as if it were an extension of his body. Unlike on the race track, he wasn't in any hurry down here. They drove miles upon miles on backcountry roads, surrounded by grassland and farmland, their only company cows and horses and an occasional *gaucho* on horseback.

They rode alongside a river for a while. "The Areco River,"

Roberto yelled. "Doesn't look like much but it's why the town built up around here."

Soon they came to a small town.

"San Antonio," he said. "Population twenty thousand."

In what looked like the center of town, the streets were cobblestone and the buildings traditional Colonial. Orange trees lined the street and wrought-iron gates lined many yards. In no time, they passed through the entire town and were once again in the country.

Soon, Roberto slowed and turned off the main road. "A friend of mine owns this *estancia*," he said. "He has a grove of fruit trees along the river. Let's stop there and stretch our legs."

He drove off the dirt road, stopped the bike near a tree and grabbed his pack. They walked toward the river a short distance away, laid out the blanket and sat down.

He stretched his legs out in front of him. "So how are you doing? Dealing with being adopted?"

"All right. It's starting to sink in, I think."

"I still remember the shock of finding out my mother was alive." He picked a blade of grass and tore it into thin strips.

"Why did your dad tell you she'd died?"

"He didn't want me to grow up thinking she'd rejected me. A mother rejecting a child. Doesn't feel right, does it?"

"No."

"It sounded like what happened with your mother was a bit different. She was scared. Alone."

"She still rejected me."

"She gave you up because she knew you'd have a better home." He tossed the grass away. "Are you going to try and find her?"

"Yes."

"Be careful."

"You don't think I should?"

"No, that's not what I meant." He tore off some more grass. "Finding my mother was hard on me, but not as hard as losing myself in her world."

"How do you mean?"

"When I started racing, I was hungry for her approval. I had to win. For her. And I did. Kept winning. The money poured in, along with the opportunities, the lifestyle, the women. For a long time, I forgot where I came from. Forgot *who* I am."

"And now?"

"I'm finding myself again. It feels good." He reached out and squeezed her hand.

"Right now, I'm feeling a little as if I don't know who I am."

"I know who you are. Don't lose yourself over this, Mallory. Don't let the circumstances of your birth define who you are. Or who you have become."

"That sounds like advice you need to live by, as well."

He smiled. "You are right. I do."

Suddenly, she felt the urge to learn more about her real heritage. "Teach me some Spanish."

He leaned back. "What do you want to know?"

"I'm not sure." She opened a bottle of water. "What's *che* mean? I hear that around here all the time."

"That's an Argentine thing. Like saying, 'Hey, you.' Sometimes people say it at the end of sentences, like Canadians say eh." He chuckled. "Silly, *che?*"

"What's an *estancia?*" she asked.

"A ranch."

"Tell me more."

"Actress is *actriz.* Soap opera is *novela.*"

She smiled and ducked her head. "What does *querida* mean?"

"Sweetheart. That's you." He turned toward her. "But I can think of a lot of words that describe you."

"Like what?" She knew she was flirting, but for once there was no one around to see them. It felt honest and real and so good after all the posturing they'd been doing over the last several weeks.

"*Regalo,* or *tesoro,* or *preciosa.*"

"I love the way your voice sounds. Everything you say. You could probably say, 'My bike has a flat tire,' and it would sound sexy."

"No. It wouldn't. But here's something that's definitely sexy." He reached out and touched the corner of her eye. "*Los ojos.* Your eyes," he whispered. "*Ojos de marrón chocolate.* Your eyes are like chocolate." He trailed his finger down her cheek. "*Carillo.*" To circle her lips. "*Los labios.*" Down her throat. "*La garganta.*" And back to the nape of her neck. "*La nuca.*"

As he stared at her lips, Mallory closed her eyes. "What are you thinking?"

"What I'd like to do to you."

"Tell me. In Spanish."

"*Quieriera besar tus labios, tu nuca, por todas partes, repetidamente.*" He said every word slowly, drawing each one out. "*Hacer el amor, toda la noche, muchas veces.*" And as he finished, his words hung before her like a fire, drawing her toward his heat.

"Whatever you said sounded wonderful," she whispered.

"It would *feel* better. Much…better."

She looked into his eyes, her heart racing. "Then what are you waiting for?"

He leaned over her and pressed his mouth to hers, ran his tongue along her lips, then delved inside her mouth, taking, demanding. Then he pressed her back to the hard ground and kissed her jawline, her throat. He was gentle but insistent, making it clear what he wanted. And what he wanted was everything she was willing to give. At this moment, she would have given him her entire body, her soul, her life.

Surprising her, he pulled back, resting his forehead against hers, his breath coming in short pants and buffeting her cheek. "We have one problem," he whispered. "You don't know what I said. Or understand the permission you granted."

"I don't care."

"Yes, you do." He flopped onto his back and closed his eyes. "More amazingly, so do I."

She was aching for him, wanting him so badly. She couldn't help but feel hurt that he'd turned away. "Here we go again. I am the only woman Roberto Castillo actually said no to."

"You don't understand." He shook his head, but he wouldn't open his eyes.

"You don't want me."

"Oh, *querida*. I do want you." He drew her into his arms, tucked her close. "I want you more than anything, anyone."

"But?"

"Not like this. Outside. Like two immature teenagers. Not here. Not now."

Not ever. She heard it in his voice. He was a good man and he didn't want to hurt her. Because he didn't love her. So why did she so badly wish to suffer? "Can we go home now?" she whispered, holding back the tears.

By the time they made it back, it was dark. Roberto drove the bike right into the garage and hopped off. Mallory was quiet. He understood.

She, on the other hand, didn't.

She handed him her helmet and he opened his mouth to speak, but stopped. How could he know what to say if he didn't know what he was feeling? If the feelings were so strange, so different, he had no way of naming them. How could he explain that down at the river she'd wanted—deserved—something from him that he couldn't give? Sex was something he'd given and taken his whole life. It was simple, uncomplicated, especially for a man.

Making love, on the other hand, was something entirely different, something Roberto had never experienced, wasn't sure he wanted to experience. He wasn't entirely sure making love was something of which he was capable.

As they headed toward the house, the sound of music hung in the warm night air.

"What is that?"

"My father. Too much *vino*." He chuckled. "He's dancing."

"Where?"

"On the patio."

"That sounds fun." Her smile was sad, lonely, but there was joy there, too, from such a small thing.

"Watch out. *Papá* will have you on your feet and in his arms in no time."

They went through the back entrance and Roberto put together some platters of grapes, plums, cold meat and *fainá,* a thin, chickpea flour bread, on their way through the kitchen. Then they made their way through the house toward the back patio.

In typical Luis fashion, he'd opened the doors wide, turned on a CD of traditional Spanish music—salsa, mambo, fandango—and had invited the entire staff and their families for an impromptu party.

Luis noticed them the moment they stepped outside. "Roberto! Mallory! It's about time you make it to your own party." He laughed. "A celebration for your last night here." He bid them to sit at one of the tables that had been set up outside while he poured them each a glass of wine.

While Mallory was watching the dancing, Roberto sat down, took a thin slice of meat, setting it atop a chunk of *fainá,* and handed it to her. Then he did the same for himself and popped it into his mouth.

One of the farmhands was performing a traditional fandango with his wife. He carried a tambourine and she a set of maracas as they performed the courtship dance of advance and retreat without touching.

When it came to an end, Mallory clapped enthusiastically and the couple bowed. Luis changed the music to a feisty mambo, and four or five little children joined in the fun. Luis held out his hand for Emilia, their cook. Her husband had died several years back, and Roberto wouldn't be surprised if his father actually married for the first time in his life.

Mallory leaned over and whispered, "Luis is a good dancer."

"Don't tell him that. It'll go to his head." He popped a small handful of grapes into his mouth.

Mallory had no sooner finished eating than Luis came over to their table. "Mallory, will you make an old man's night by dancing with him?"

"Only if you'll teach me to tango."

"That, I can do. It's one of the easiest dances."

"Then let's go." She smiled and took his hand.

Roberto sat back with his glass of wine and watched. From the time he was a little boy, he'd listened to his father teach people to dance. Roberto could imagine every word he was saying to Mallory.

I lead. I lead. Don't look at your feet. Look at me. No, no, bring your foot to the inside. And always, *To tango, the most important thing is to feel the music. If you are true to the music, there are no mistakes.*

Roberto couldn't take his eyes off Mallory. The way her eyes sparkled in the candlelight as she laughed at his father's instructions. The way she held herself. She was a natural, moving fluidly and confidently, not stiffly or formally as he'd expected. She was a part of the music. He had little doubt that when she searched for her birth parents she was going to confirm she had Hispanic blood.

The song ended and Mallory and his father came back to the table. "This old man is tired," Luis said, sitting down. "But you? You are young and dance like an angel." He kissed Mallory's hand.

"Thank you. You're a wonderful teacher, a marvelous dancer."

"Hmm. Roberto's a better dancer than I am."

Roberto shook his head.

"Can you tango?" Mallory asked.

"Of course he can." Luis laughed. "Go. Show her."

"Will you dance with me, Roberto?" She was playing with fire. And they were both going to get burned.

So be it. He stood, held out his hand and led her away from the table. "I warn you," he whispered while they waited for the music to begin. "I'm nowhere near as polite as my father where a tango is concerned."

"What does that mean?"

"I'm giving you an out. I won't hold it against you if you walk off the floor."

"Dancing is dancing."

"You think so?"

Quiet, charming music filled the night air. Roberto slowly drew Mallory into his arms. Not too close. This was one of his favorite dances. The guitar started out slowly, the accordion and violin joined, building the emotion. He kept it simple, and, to her credit, Mallory kept pace, step for step.

"Get ready," he said.

"For what?"

"This."

The tempo dramatically quickened, and he swung her outward, only to tug her back to his chest. Now, he held her as tightly as possible, moving their two bodies as one. Her breath was on his neck, her chest pressed against him. She was his, moving where he wanted, when he wanted, molding herself to him.

"You're right," she whispered on a shaky breath. "You dance much differently than your father."

As if to prove his point, he spun her again and then yanked her back to him, pulling her hard against him. Then the music quieted, turned romantic, and he compensated with little steps, footwork that took them side to side. She rested her forehead against his cheek. His body was on fire.

The music built. "Here it is again," he said.

This time, he could tell by the harmony in their steps that she could feel it, that she read him and the music. Holding her tight, he turned his face into her, closed his eyes and breathed her in. The subtle scent of grass clung to her skin, and, though the wind from their motorcycle ride still clung to her hair, the sweet scent of honey still lingered. She moved as if she'd been carved for his arms, for his body.

"Can you feel what you do to me?" he whispered. "Do you still think I don't want you?"

He pressed against the small of her back, intimately connecting their hips. She sucked in a breath and her head fell back, exposing her long, beautiful neck.

As the music reached its final crescendo, Robert dipped her back and, instinctively, she brought a leg up to wrap around him, joining them intimately at the hips. By the time the music faded to silence, the world around them had vanished. Her eyes, her lips, her neck. She was all he could see. All he could feel, smell.

Their gazes locked, and the raw and true desire reflected in her eyes startled him. Roberto suddenly remembered where they were. He glanced around. They were completely alone. His father, Emilia, the *gauchos,* the children. Everyone had gone. They'd flicked off the inside lights. Only candles on the tables and the stars and moon in the sky illuminated the night.

"You are probably thinking I planned this," he murmured.

"Did you?"

"Some things are better left to chance." He bent and kissed her throat. He couldn't help it. But when her answering moan vibrated through him, stirring long-dormant desires, he pulled away while he still could. "We can't do this."

She touched his cheek and made him look at her. "You're afraid I'll hurt you. That's it, isn't it?"

Finally, she understood what he couldn't seem to accept. He turned, his heart racing, his skin on fire.

"Roberto." She stepped in front of him, touched her fingertips to his lips. "Make love to me."

The French doors to his bedroom were twenty steps away. Twenty steps to heaven. His body ached for her. He could no longer resist. Swiftly picking her up, he carried her across the floor, double-time. Threw the doors open and stepped into the dark stillness of his bedroom.

He kicked the doors shut behind them. It was black except for moonlight and the faint flicker of the patio candles shimmering through glass. She ran her hands through his hair, and for once he didn't think to pull away. He wanted her hands on him, everywhere.

She walked to his bed and deliberately unbuttoned her shirt.

He moved toward her and stilled her hands. "Mallory, stop." This was uncharted territory for him, and he was worried he would slip into old, comfortable patterns. "You've been right about me. I...do things to...distance myself from women."

"I know," she whispered, letting her top slip to the floor.

He touched her bare shoulder. "I don't want to do that to you."

"You won't."

"How do you know?" He pulled his hand back. Maybe it was

in his blood, maybe he couldn't help but hurt her. "I'm not sure I can be who you need me to be."

"I only want you to be who you are."

She accepted him. *Him*. His heart pounded first with fear and then joy. *"Si hacemos esto, Mallory, vas a ser mía."* He had to warn her. "If we do this, you'll be mine."

"I already am," she whispered.

"GOODBYE, LUIS." Mallory hugged Roberto's father. "Thank you for everything."

"Anytime you want another glass of the best wine in Argentina, you come and visit us, Mallory." Roberto's father smiled with genuine, heartfelt emotion. "With or without my son."

Standing beside them, next to the airstrip, Roberto watched the exchange with a deep sense of gratification. His father liked Mallory without reservation. That was good. Even so, Roberto was struck with an overwhelming sense of apprehension. Last night with Mallory, their last night here, had been, at once, amazing and frightening.

He hadn't had sex with Mallory. He'd made love with a woman for the first time in his life. Made love. Not only had she declared she belonged to him, she'd gone on to show it with every tender, insistent and frenzied touch of her hands.

There was now no doubt in his mind he deeply cared for this woman. But could he be hers? Wholly? Completely? Could he surrender to her, trust her? Believe in her the way she believed in him?

She turned toward Roberto with those beautiful brown eyes and he was filled with only the most tender of affections, until he remembered how she'd touched him last night, and passion, deep and consuming, stoked that warmth to fire. Maybe if they stayed here in Argentina and let the rest of the world roll on by. His races, her shows. Maybe if they insulated themselves, they'd have a chance together.

"Are you ready?" she asked.

To face the world again? Not even close. But he didn't have a choice. He had obligations, people counting on him. He took a deep breath and one last look out over his land, unsure of when he'd be back again.

"Give me a few minutes, would you, *querida?*" He touched her cheek. "Then we'll be off."

With one last look around, she climbed the steps to the jet, leaving Roberto alone with his father.

"Something is troubling you," Luis said. "What is it?"

Roberto had vowed long, long ago to never ask his father's opinion on Roberto's romantic entanglements. There had never before been a point. He'd known what his father would've said. Besides, Roberto had never been serious about any of the women he'd been with in the past, so Luis would've only been wasting his breath.

This time, with a sense of desperation, Roberto said, "I need to know what you think, *Papá.*"

"About what?"

"Mallory."

His father glanced over at him with a surprised look on his face. "You are asking me? About a woman?"

Roberto nodded.

"How would I know, Roberto? I know nothing of your life. Nothing of the kind of woman who would fit in your life."

"You know me."

"Do I?"

"I haven't changed as much as you might think. Only adapted."

"Is that what you call it?" His father glanced at him skeptically. "The partying, gambling, womanizing?"

"Playing a part, *Papá*. That's all. The Roberto you know was here all the time. Inside."

"So you are done with all that now? Had enough of that life?"

Roberto nodded.

"In that case, I say *finally!*" His father looked away for a moment. When he spoke his voice was quiet and soft. "Your Mallory seems honest, compassionate. I'm guessing from her level of success, she's a hard worker. There's not much more I can tell after only a few days. But from the way she looks at you,

Roberto, you are her sun, moon and stars. What more can you ask for from a woman? What more do you need?"

"I don't doubt she cares for me," Roberto said, looking away. "But how do you trust? How do you let a woman…hold your heart in her hands?"

"You just do. Because a life without love means nothing."

That wasn't the answer he was looking for.

"Every weekend in your race car," his father said, "you risk everything. Don't tell me you can't face the possibility of a broken heart."

"What if a man loves a woman so much, *Papá,* that the pain of death would pale in comparison to living without her?"

"Well, then, there is the answer. If a man does not trust, he will *definitely* be living without love." His father reached up and rubbed Roberto's head. "*Un sueño.* You have a dream waiting for you. You brought home a *good* woman, who *deserves* you. And you, my lovely son, deserve her."

Roberto closed his eyes and leaned into his father's touch.

"Prove it, Roberto. To yourself. To her. Step inside your dream. And open your heart."

CHAPTER TWENTY-ONE

SHE WAS GORGEOUS. Flat-out, drop-dead gorgeous.

Outside at the charity benefit, standing on an immaculately manicured lawn, Roberto glanced past the sea of faces and took his time studying the woman. Long blond hair, ocean-blue eyes, lips that looked as soft as angel feathers and a body that had obviously been artificially designed for one thing and one thing only—sex.

Her gaze intent on him, she walked across the grass, purpose plastered all over that perfectly made-up face. "Aren't you that race car driver?"

"That depends. Do you like drivers?"

"Absolutely." She stepped close. Too close. A picture of this woman could've been stamped next to the word *siren* in the dictionary. "This thing is getting boring. All these long drawn-out speeches. All these do-gooders patting themselves on the back. How 'bout we liven things up?"

"What do you have in mind?"

"Come into my house and I'll show you," she whispered, turning toward the dais at the front and pretending to listen to the man who was speaking. "That's my husband." She nodded toward the podium. "He loves hearing himself talk. I'd say we have at least a half an hour before he shuts up and starts looking for me."

Roberto laughed. "Where do I go and when?"

"Two minutes after I leave go through the doors at the patio level. I'll be inside. Waiting for you." She headed toward the house and entered through the upper level.

Roberto waited the requisite amount of time before heading

toward the house. He stepped inside and there the bombshell was as planned, behind the bar mixing them both martinis.

She handed one to him. "Cheers!"

He set it down without tasting it and pulled her into his arms. "We don't have a lot of time. Let's not waste it."

"Sounds like a plan." She set down her glass and wrapped her arms around his neck. When she reached for his hair, he grabbed her wrists and kissed her, as they backed into the wall.

This was every man's dream. The thrill, the spontaneity, the forbidden nature of the attraction. As hot as this woman was, he should've felt at least the stirrings of excitement.

Instead, he felt sick. Disgusted with himself. It was all he could do to keep kissing this woman, keep touching her, keep acting as if she turned him on. He gripped her side, felt her taut abs, her curves. And wasn't the least bit moved. His hands shook, which she probably took for attraction because it seemed to energize her. She drew him closer, pushing herself into him and hooking a leg around him.

Mallory stood watching Roberto kissing Kristin, stared at the way Kristin's leg wrapped around Roberto, and all she wanted to do was get away as fast as her legs would carry her. But she was stuck. The cameras were rolling. This was Roberto's last cameo for *Racing Hearts* and, as far as Mallory was concerned, it was one too many.

Her brain wrapped itself around the image in front of her, seeing Roberto's hand on Kristin's back, and all she could do was remember all the different ways he'd touched her their last night in Argentina. She loved him. But could he ever love only her?

The assistant director signaled to her, but Mallory couldn't move. His hands moved silently and frantically, trying to get her attention.

I know. I know. I'm supposed to be acting in this scene.

At this point, Mallory didn't have to bother. All she had to do was imagine that kiss had been real.

She stepped forward onto the set. "Well, isn't this lovely," she managed to say past the lump forming in her throat.

Roberto spun around and jerked his hands away as if his skin was burning. "I can explain."

Betrayal, misery, anger. Disgust. She couldn't help the emotions. They'd welled up inside like a geyser, blocking out her lines. She forced herself to glance at the prompter and gathered herself, pushed aside her emotions and let something cool and controlled take hold.

"I'd like to see you try," she said, putting her hands on her hips and walking toward them. "Because I have a feeling this is exactly what Kristin was planning all along when she asked me to meet her in the house at…" She glanced at her wristwatch. "Eleven o'clock."

"You caught me," Kristin said with a smirk. "You always were the smart one." She stalked past Mallory and went back off the set.

Roberto took a step toward Mallory.

"Don't!" She put her hands up to stop him. Now she had to muster every acting bone in her body. If she ever had to push him away in real life, it would kill her.

"It didn't mean anything," he said.

"I'm sure it didn't. Nothing ever does with Kristin."

"I'm sorry," he said.

"So am I," she said. "I thought we were something special."

"Were?"

"We're done. That's it. Finished. It's over."

"No second chances?"

"It was fun while it lasted, Roberto. And I don't regret leaving Shane. But…goodbye." Mallory made herself turn and walk away.

"Cut!" the director shouted. "That was awesome. First take. You guys were great. Very believable."

Mallory took a deep breath, trying to whisk that scene resolutely from her mind. *It wasn't real. It wasn't real.* It was merely one more step in expanding her character. She turned around, trying to smile.

Roberto held her gaze, looking uncomfortable and awkward.

"I have to admit," she said, "you did that so well, it bothered me."

"Well, if I don't win a race pretty soon, I guess I could always turn to acting."

"Yes, you probably could." She suddenly felt sad. "That's it, though. We're done with your last cameo. I'll miss having you on the set."

"So is your character going to rebound with someone else on *Racing Hearts?* You have another hot kiss in your horizon."

"Jealous?" She grinned, before remembering how terrible she'd just felt.

He looked as if he needed to sit down.

"Hey." Mallory touched his arm. "Are you okay?"

"No," he said. "That was awful. One of the worst experiences of my life."

"It was a scene. It didn't mean anything. I'll go find you some water."

She found a cooler near the break table. On her way back, she stopped when she noticed the actress who played Kristin, the one who'd seduced Roberto in the last scene, sauntering toward Roberto. "That was kinda fun," Mallory's costar said. "Anytime you want to hook up for real, Roberto, give me a call."

"Never gonna happen."

"Because of Mallory?"

"Yeah." He nodded. "Because of Mallory."

Because of her. Mallory smiled. Maybe there was hope for them yet.

"I CANNOT BELIEVE the studio rewrote Roberto's cameos," Theo said, clearly irate. "Patricia was almost ready to sue the studio." The waiter walked away after taking their lunch order, and Theo leaned forward, resting his elbows on the table. "I have to admit, I'm glad we're done with him. Now we can orchestrate some quiet way to announce that you two are over and done, and get to work repairing your image. You, of course, are the one who broke it off with him. We need to do this before he gets any ideas about seeing other women."

"He's not going to be seeing anyone else."

"This is Roberto Castillo we're talking about. Fake or not, this is the longest-standing relationship he's ever had. I'd say any day now he'll be calling it quits. We need to do it first. Break up before he does. Before he breaks your heart."

It was nice that he cared, but this was her personal life. "No."

Theo glanced at her as if he hadn't heard right, but didn't say anything.

"I'm not calling it off with Roberto," Mallory said, glancing at him.

Theo shook his head. "You planned all this, didn't you? The casino, Mexico, Argentina, the changes to Roberto's cameos. You wanted that part all along."

"Yes. I did."

"I'm impressed." He steepled his fingers. "But you're little plan came with a big consequence, so I hope you're satisfied. You lost the part in the romantic comedy."

Maybe the pendulum had swung too far to the other side.

"You want to know why?"

No, but she was sure he was going to tell her.

"Because you took the part in *Three Sisters*," he said, almost as though he were delighting in rubbing it in. "You chose a silly indie flick over the opportunity to be involved in a possible box office blockbuster."

"I don't care, Theo. I want to act. I want to enjoy my job." Suddenly, it hit her. "You're not really worried about Roberto breaking my heart. All you care about is what he's doing to my image, and you only care about my image because you want to maximize the money."

"I'm an agent, Mallory. It's what I do."

She set her fork down and sat up straighter. This was it. She either drew a line in the sand or forever dealt with him. "You've been calling the shots since the beginning, but I was only twenty years old. I appreciate everything you've done for me. I wouldn't be where I am today without you. But things have changed. I've changed. I don't need or want you to dictate every move I make. Not anymore. I'm calling the shots in my career from now on. And my personal life is my own business."

"You're an actress, Mallory. You can't separate personal from public."

"I can try."

He took a sip of ice water, set the glass down and sat back in his chair. "Well, I don't work that way. I make stars, Mallory. I made you. You want me as your agent, then I call the shots. You don't want me to call the shots, then you'd better find a new agent."

"All right, then." She set her napkin on the table and stood. "Our relationship is terminated."

CHAPTER TWENTY-TWO

THE MOMENT ROBERTO OPENED the door to his Manhattan apartment the scent of candles burning and the sound of soft jazz music wafted toward him from the bedroom. He paused, looked again at the number on the door and, seeing he definitely had the correct place, went inside. Someone, he was guessing a someone of the female gender, had managed to get into his apartment.

Mallory. He smiled at the thought. She knew he was going to be getting in late tonight. But candles and music? That didn't sound like her. Then again, they hadn't been able to work in seeing each other since his last cameo on *Racing Hearts*. Maybe she'd missed him as much as he'd missed her.

He threw his keys on the foyer table and tossed his jacket on the huge sectional sofa on the way toward the bedroom. A champagne bottle on ice and a glass flute sat on the bedside table. The covers were turned down on the big king-size bed and he could hear water running in the bathroom. Thinking he'd surprise her in the shower, he quickly unbuttoned his shirt and let it drop to the floor.

The water shut off. Dammit. Then the bathroom door opened and he turned. Wrapped in a towel, her silhouette was backlit by the bright bathroom lights. "Mal—" He stopped. It wasn't her. "Kacy?" *Son of a—* "How did you get in here?" He tugged his shirt back on and buttoned it up.

"You'd be surprised what a doorman will do for the promise of some action." Weaving slightly, she strolled toward the bed, poured him a flute of bubbly and held it out. Drunk again. "Besides, I'm Kacy Haughton. What am I going to do, rob you?"

Roberto was going to shred that doorman like rubber on rough track. Glancing around the room, he took the glass from her hand and set it back down on the table. Apparently they were alone, so her objective couldn't have been more photos.

"What are you doing here?" he asked.

"I've been watching you and Mallory in the news. Everyone says you've been fighting again. I thought—"

"You thought wrong." He headed for the door.

"Roberto." She grabbed his arm.

"Kacy, you are making a fool of yourself. I'm going to leave this room and shut the door. You have five minutes to get dressed and hit the road before I call the police."

"You wouldn't do that."

"Try me."

"Roberto, we could be good together."

"No. We can't."

"How 'bout this, then?" She set her hands on her hips. "I'm pregnant. And you're the father."

His stomach flipped. That was one statement he'd dreaded hearing for the last decade or more. Now he almost wished he was the father. He'd get custody of that child so fast Kacy's head would spin. "Kacy, I hate to break it to you, but I can't be the father of your child. It's biologically impossible."

"Nothing's impossible."

"You getting pregnant with my child is. Especially since we have never had sex."

"How can you say that?" She truly looked hurt. "We've slept together several times."

"As in slept in the same bed. And only once. You were obviously too drunk to remember anything."

"You're lying. The way I remember it, the sex was incredible."

"Goes to show how vivid your imagination can be."

"Well, I'm not imagining this." She tugged on her bath towel, threatening to drop it.

He closed his eyes. "Go, Kacy. Leave. Now. I have tried to be polite, but I have had enough."

"Roberto—" She sounded scared, but he refused to open his eyes and look at her. "Okay. I'm sorry. The truth is…you…you were the only…the only man I could think of who might actually care." He sensed her in front of him. She rested her head on his chest and wrapped her arms around him. "Please. I don't know what else to do. Who else to go to."

The door to his condo closed, and his eyes popped open the exact second Mallory stepped into the hall. He stood, frozen to the spot, coherent thought suddenly deserting him.

With a smile on her face, Mallory walked toward the bedroom. "Rob—Roberto?"

"Mallory, this isn't what it looks like." He set Kacy aside and walked toward her.

Spinning around, Mallory ran back toward the door.

"Mallory, *detente!* Give me a minute to explain."

"No! I can't take this. The constant doubt. About you. About me." She turned, held the doorknob in her hand. "It's always going to be something. Someone." She raced out of the apartment, slamming the door behind her.

Roberto ran after her. The moment he opened the door, the elevator closed. He raked his hands through his hair, debating on whether or not he could catch her outside. And then what? Would she listen? Would she believe him? Maybe today, but what about tomorrow? There was always going to be something or someone threatening to tear them apart.

He walked slowly into his apartment and fell back against the foyer wall. This had to have been a bad dream. He looked around. No, he was really here and the woman he loved had just walked out on him. And he couldn't blame her.

Loved. He did love her. And his father's words finally made sense. Roberto had to let go. He had to trust Mallory. He had to trust this woman was not his mother.

Kacy, now thankfully dressed, came toward him.

"Don't." He held out his hand, making sure she couldn't come near him. "You have done enough damage."

"Go after her. You have to go after her and explain."

"There's no point. She's gone."

"I'm sorry," Kacy whispered, sounding more sincere than Roberto had ever known her to be. "I didn't mean for that... I didn't know..."

"Are you really pregnant?"

She nodded. "Yes." Her voice was small, frightened.

"Then you need help."

"I know," she cried, tears streaming down her face.

"Your family?"

"No."

"Will you go to a treatment facility if I take you?"

She hesitated and then nodded. "But first, I want to talk to Mallory and tell her the truth."

"No," he whispered. It was one of the hardest things he'd ever had to say. "She has to find her way to the truth. All on her own."

"I'm NOT SURE what was the last straw. That final *Racing Hearts* cameo. Or Argentina." Patricia had flown in to New York to have, as she'd called it, "a come-to-Pat meeting." She'd met him for lunch and then proceeded to chew his butt over dessert. "Everyone's assuming you were sleeping together. Were you? Before this whole Kacy fiasco?"

"That's none of your business, Patricia."

Silently, she studied him for a moment. "The point is, you've corrupted America's Sweetheart and the public may never forgive you."

He glanced down at the latest tabloid nightmare and shook his head. *Kacy Haughton In Rehab Over Roberto Castillo!* The next one: *Secret Lovers! Roberto And Kacy, Pregnant?* And the last: *America's Sweetheart With A Side Of Bitter!*

"This bad press is killing you."

"No, Patricia. It's killing my *image.* Not me. They can say whatever they want on the news and in the papers and the fact is, it doesn't do a damned thing to me personally. Because I don't care anymore."

"Well, the Grossos still do." She threw her napkin on the

table. "You know, this whole thing is fixable. As soon as Mallory finds out the truth about Kacy and how you helped her get into rehab, called Kacy's family and smoothed things over, she'll think you're a prince and forgive you in a heartbeat."

Yes, she would. She belonged to him. She'd said it. She'd accepted it. She loved him. Now, if she could only take one last step. And believe in him.

"Go to her, Roberto. Tell her the truth."

"No."

"She called me, you know. Asked me to represent her."

Bueno. "Theo's a jerk." At least her professional life was coming together. "What did you say?"

"That I don't represent actresses, but I'd get some names for her."

"Find someone who'll take care of her, *che?*"

Silent for a moment, Patricia studied him. "You're in love with her, aren't you? Really, honestly and truly in love with her."

He wanted Mallory there waiting for him at the end of every race. He felt good, like a good man, when he was with her. He could be with her anywhere—Las Vegas, Paris, Charlotte—but as long as she was with him, any place in the world would feel like home. All of those feelings surprised him, but not as much as wanting to be in her life. He wanted to see her play the lead in a movie. He was proud of her and her accomplishments. He wanted to protect her as much as he wanted to be there to catch her if she stumbled and fell.

It took what had happened with Kacy to make him realize that Mallory was all that mattered. And he was right for her. He could be who she needed. He wouldn't push her away. Already, his heart was breaking, but if she were here in front of him, right now, he would want nothing more than to open his arms, let her in and love her.

"Yes," Roberto said, swallowing past the tight lump in his throat. "I am in love with her."

"Then ask her to marry you, you idiot. She will. I know she will." Patricia grinned. "I can see it now. Ask her during an interview. Or better yet, at one of the races. That's perfect. The fans will go crazy over it."

"No."

"Just think ab—"

"Dammit, Patricia," he said. "I'm sick of living my life out in the press. Don't you get it?" He stood and paced. "That's it. No more cameos. No more commercials, interviews, magazine spreads or high-profile charity events. From now on my contracts will include the minimum requirements from a publicity stand-point. I don't care how much less they pay me. I'm living my life. The way I want to live it. And if the Grossos don't want to renew my contract, I'll find someone else who will. From now on, my career will succeed or fail based on my driving record. Period. Or I'll be retiring from racing."

Patricia sat back in her chair.

"And if you can't live with that, I'll find another agent who can."

"Okay." She sighed. "I get it. You're stepping off the roulette wheel."

"Yes," he said. "Once and for all."

"A win, or at least placing in the top ten for a while, would make negotiating a lot easier."

He glared at her.

"All right. All right." She shook her head. "I suppose this means a house in the 'burbs, kids and a van. The whole shebang."

"I should be so lucky."

CHAPTER TWENTY-THREE

"YOU DON'T NEED to win this, Roberto, to prove a point." One hundred and seventy-five laps into the two-hundred-lap race at Pocono, Harry's voice came through Roberto's helmet in waves of calm. "You hear me?"

"Yeah, I hear you," Roberto said, punching it down on the straightaway as he approached Turn Two.

This triangular track was unlike any other track he'd ever raced. With low banking on the turns, it wasn't like driving on a normal superspeedway.

"Remember. You got the pole position with a track qualifying record. You were the one who set the pace today. You've been in first place most of the race. No one's going to doubt you again. Okay?"

No, it wasn't okay. He *could* win. Therefore, he *needed* to win. He needed to prove to the Grossos they hadn't made a mistake in signing him on.

Being as he was used to steeply banked turns, this track should've thrown him. Instead, he'd found his groove early on, thrilled at the feeling of the straightaways and, probably most important of all, his team had the car running the best it had all season. That'd been a challenge, too, at this track, setting up the chassis to perform both on the straightaways and the tight turns.

"Stay loose. You've got second place locked."

Trey Sanford was currently in first, and Roberto knew he could take him. All day, he'd been jockeying back and forth with Kent. They might be teammates, but both Roberto and Kent wanted to win this race.

For who? His thoughts ricocheted around in his head like popcorn in a microwave. *For Madre? No.* He was all done racing for her. *For Mallory?* He knew she was here. Her parents had parked their motor home in the infield campground, and he could feel her presence, like a balm. She was there. Watching. Thinking. Hating him? Loving him? He was going to get her back, some way, somehow. But he wasn't racing for her today, either. *So why the hell are you here?*

"Two to go," his spotter said.

"Tell the guys," Roberto said, "they did a kick-ass job on this car."

"You can tell them yourself."

He was coming out of Turn Three. "I'll meet them in Victory Lane." Roberto punched it down. With the approach to Turn One he had time to make a move. And, most important, he had the power.

Kent was on his tail, pushing. They passed Trey Sanford and the finish line, providing Cargill-Grosso Racing with their first one-two finish of the season.

"Woohoo!" Harry yelled.

A momentary thrill raced through Roberto. With every race, he was understanding stock car racing better and better, but, more important, he'd broken his dry spell. The season would go better from here on out. He was on the right track. Finally.

He spun in circles, burned rubber for the fans and then took off for Victory Lane. His team was waiting for him when he hopped out of the car. Slaps on the back, hugs, whoops. Harry was the most excited Roberto had ever seen him. Everyone was happy. Even Nathan Cargill came out to congratulate Roberto. Dean and Patsy seemed to put aside their preoccupation with finding their daughter and joined in the excitement.

The crowd loosened, parted a bit and Kent came toward him. "You did it, man! All by yourself."

"No." Roberto gave him a quick hug. "I did it *with* you."

"You deserved that win. With or without me."

Patsy came up to him, a wry smile on her face. "Well, you

made Dean happy today. But Argentina? Have you heard anything I've been saying to you?"

He nodded.

Patsy studied him for a minute. "My God. You're in love with her, aren't you?"

He nodded again.

"Well, then," she said on a sigh. "There's only one thing you can do about that."

"I'm not sure she'll have me."

Patsy laughed. "And all this time I thought you knew women." She gave him a quick hug and stepped back into the crowd.

That's when Roberto saw his mother's face amidst the sea of faces. She was smiling, finally happy with him that he'd won a race. He could hear her saying to everyone around her, "That's my boy. My son, Roberto Castillo Franco." And no sense of pride infused him because of her.

She squeezed through the throngs of people in the hopes of getting close to him. In the past, he would've reached out for her, wanting her in the limelight with him, so that she could gloat about him back home in Buenos Aires with her family. Today, Roberto didn't care whether she made it to him or not. In fact, he was sure he wouldn't care if she never came to another race.

Biologically, she'd always be his mother, but, he realized in that moment, she'd never hold a mother's place in his heart. Never. "Roberto!" she said, drawing his gaze. Their eyes caught, and she stopped pushing against the crowd. She could see it on his face. He didn't hate her, he didn't love her. She simply didn't matter. Today's race had been for him. And no one else.

He glanced around at all the smiling, joyous faces in the crowd and there, four or five people back, he saw a very familiar face. *"Papá!"* he yelled, reaching out.

His father joined him with his team. "I guess I came to the right race, *che.*" They hugged. "I'm very proud of you, Roberto," he whispered in his ear.

Roberto squeezed him tightly and then let go. "How did you get here?"

"Mallory sent me tickets. Met me at the airport and sat with me during the entire race. She said you wanted me here, though I had my doubts." Luis's smile disappeared. "I hope it's okay that I came."

Roberto nodded, overcome with emotion. She knew him better than he knew himself. "It's more than okay. It's perfect." He scanned the crowd, looking for her. He couldn't wait to hold her. "Where is she, *Papá?* Where'd she go?"

"She went home."

"Home?"

"To New York."

"Did she see the end of the race?"

"Yes." His father nodded. "She cried. Happy tears for you."

As Roberto's excitement abruptly abated, microphones were shoved in front of his face and questions were asked and answered. He posed for pictures with his team. Flashes flashed. People cheered. The revelry continued long past the time Roberto felt any enthusiasm over his win. Finally, the crowd loosened. The last of the reporters and cameramen had left.

He rejoined his father and asked, "You ready to head home?"

"To Manhattan?"

"Yes."

His father hesitated. "Well, you know me and big cities. I stayed with Mallory's parents in their motor home last night. If it's all right with you, I'll stay there a few more days."

"Okay, *Papá.* Call me."

His father nodded and took off toward the campground.

Kent slapped Roberto on the back. "This is a biggie for you. We should celebrate."

"No." Roberto shook his head. "I'm out of here."

"Hot plans tonight?"

"Yep. That's it." Roberto faked as convincing a grin as he could muster. "Sizzling plans."

MALLORY HEADED through the stands to the parking lot and watched the image of Roberto celebrating on the monitors, too cried-out to shed another single tear. He'd won. She was so happy for him. This would change the tide for his career in NASCAR, she was sure of it. He was going to be okay.

Or was he?

She studied his motions. He was doing that thing with his head, tilting it to the right with a smile pasted on his face. Anyone else watching him would've thought he couldn't be any happier about this win. Only there was more to the story. He was obviously proud of his team, proud of the race he'd run, but something was bothering him.

Guilt, maybe. Shame over what had happened between him and Kacy. Was the man finally developing a conscience? She'd given herself to him in Argentina. Wholly and completely. Recklessly. And he'd broken her heart. After all this time trying to believe otherwise, Theo had been right. She was a notch on Roberto's bedpost.

No. That couldn't be true. She refused to believe it, not after remembering their last night in Argentina. That night he'd given to her something he'd never given to another woman. Ever. He'd given himself.

Back on the TV a reporter asked Roberto a question, and he glanced into the camera as if he was looking right at her. The expression on his face at that moment wasn't all that different from when she'd found him at his apartment with Kacy Haughton.

"I don't understand," she whispered. "How could you do it?"

He couldn't have, her heart answered. *He didn't.*

How many lies had she seen with her own eyes these past months? The Roberto she knew would never have been with Kacy Haughton. *So who the hell is Roberto Castillo really? And what are you going to believe? What you see or what you know in your heart?*

ROBERTO SAT at the dark end of the polished wooden bar and stared at the glass of Chivas on the rocks. A drink would settle his nerves. Maybe he should buy a whole bottle, take it home with him and settle a lot of nerves. Something about forgetting everything and not feeling anything at this particular moment sounded damned good.

He brought the glass to his lips, and the smell, pungent and thick, made him stop. This wasn't going to do him any good. The truth was, as much as it hurt, he didn't want to forget a single thing about Mallory. He closed his eyes and put her together, piece by piece, in his mind. He imagined her talking, laughing, touching him.

He'd fallen in love for the first and last time in his life. It was almost funny that after all the years of trying to prove otherwise he truly was a one-woman man.

He pushed away the drink, slapped down a bill and walked the several blocks to his apartment building. He nodded to the doorman and the security guard jumped up the moment Roberto's shoes hit the marble flooring. "Mr. Castillo," he said, practically falling all over himself. "I want to apologize for letting your friend—"

"That's okay. You did the right thing." He'd told the building management that he didn't want the man fired. Kacy had done enough damage already.

"That's what I figured." The man breathed a sigh of relief. "She was pretty upset tonight—"

"Tonight? You let a woman up to my floor tonight?"

"Yes, sir. She said this was really important."

Kacy must've skipped out on treatment. "Son of a bitch."

"Mr. Castillo—"

"Never mind." Roberto stalked off to the elevators, went to his floor and pushed open the door to his apartment. At the first sign of candlelight in his living room, his shoulders sagged. "Dammit, Kacy, I'm too tired for this." He strode through his foyer. "Get the hell out of my apartment. Now. Before I call the police."

When there was no response, he stepped farther into the living room and spotted a feminine figure on his balcony. Jeans and T-shirt. So not like Kacy. This woman was too full-figured, too curvy. *Mallory*. No, his mind had to be playing tricks on him. He took another few steps. It *was* her. She was looking outward across the city and apparently couldn't hear him above the sounds of the city.

He swallowed down the lump welling in his throat, trying to think of what to say, what to do, knowing so much rode on what happened right here, right now.

She'd come to him, he reminded himself. *She'd* come to him.

Slowly, he walked across the living room and stopped at the open door to the balcony. With any luck at all, he'd have all the time in the world to thank her later for bringing his father to the race, but for now there were more important things on his mind. "Mallory?"

She spun around. Her expression was serious, too serious for a straightforward making-up.

"I wasn't sure I'd ever see you again." Tentatively, he walked toward her, opening his arms.

"No." She held out her hands, stopping him several feet away. "I so desperately want your arms around me, but first we need to talk."

Dios. His heart sank, heavy with disappointment and resignation. "I don't want to talk."

"We have to."

"So you want an explanation? About Kacy?"

"No—"

"It's okay. I get it." He walked to the balcony rail, keeping his distance. "Back when those pictures of Kacy and me in that bar in Martinsville were published, I gave you nothing. I didn't think I needed to explain, thought I shouldn't have to." He turned and leaned against the rail. "Things are different today."

"Yes, they are."

"You have a right to know why she was here."

"That's not it." She stepped toward him. "I might have a right to know, but I don't need to know."

"But I—"

"Shh." She reached out and put her hand on his mouth, silencing him. "First, there's something I need to say."

He waited.

"It took me a while to realize that this issue would keep coming up between us until we resolved it once and for all. Until I resolved it." She went to stand next to him. "Tonight, you can no doubt explain Kacy's presence away. But next month? Next year? Someday, there will be another woman who wants, thinks she deserves a piece of *the* Roberto Castillo. You can't control what other people do."

Reaching out, she touched his chest. "I don't know why Kacy was here the other night, but I don't need you to explain. I trust with my whole heart and soul, Roberto, that you had nothing to do with her being here." She cupped his face in her hands. "I will never doubt you again."

He couldn't believe it, didn't know if he could trust what he'd just heard. But he could see it in her face. She meant every word. She saw through it all. She knew. Finally, someone had bothered to search for the real him beneath all the counterfeit layers. He could not believe that a woman could love him this much, but she did. She'd fallen in love with the man, not the driver, not the winner. She believed in the man.

His father had been right. This woman's love was perfect in every way. "Now can I hold you?" he whispered.

"Please." Smiling, she stepped between his legs.

He wrapped his arms around her, burying his face in her neck, and a calm that had eluded him for days settled over his shoulders. "Can I tell you what happened with Kacy anyway?"

"No." She chuckled.

He laughed. "Too bad. I need to get it off my chest." He quickly explained the details about how Kacy came to be naked in his apartment. "She came here, I think, because she doesn't know another soul who would have cared enough to do something to help her."

"You're a good man." Mallory leaned back and looked into his face. "She knew that."

This woman, he trusted—finally trusted—would be honest and loyal. *This* woman didn't have it in her to be cruel. "My heart, my body, my soul. You are the only woman I have ever loved, Mallory. Ever will love."

"I KNOW." Mallory looked into his eyes and understood with total clarity what he was saying. It was how she felt toward him.

He'd helped her find herself. He knew the real Mallory. "Do *you* know how much I love you?"

"I do." He nodded. "For the first time in my life, I can see myself getting married, having children, living a real life that has meaning and substance. *Quiero solamente tu amor. Tu toque. Tu pasión. Para siempre.* And the whole world is going to know it. When we walk into a room, every woman will see that you are the only one for me. Soon, and this will happen, women will pay no attention to me at all." He laughed. "And there is the interesting irony in all of this."

"How's that?"

"Someday the shoe will be on the other foot, *querida.* Your career's going to skyrocket, and men will want to be all over you. What do I do when a scene calls for you to kiss another actor? Or pretend as though you are making love with him?"

"It's a job. It's only an act."

"Doesn't matter. Other women might flirt with me, but I can guarantee you that no other woman will be touching these lips."

She hadn't thought of that.

"I don't want you to quit doing something you love. That leaves only one solution. I suck it up. I deal. And I will. *Te prometo.* Because I know you love me. *Sólo yo.* Only me. All those other men don't get you." He smiled. "You belong to me, *querida.* Like I belong to you."

"It is as easy as that, isn't it?"

"Mmm-hmm." He drew her into his arms. "Believe it. Trust it. You know me, and you know it's true."

She snuggled her face into his neck and kissed him. *The* Roberto Castillo loved her. He really did. And he was just a man, nothing more, nothing less. His image might be larger than life, but he wasn't. He hurt, he ached, he breathed, he probably cried like every other man. And when he got down on one knee in front of her, he was just a man looking into the face of the woman he loved, knowing she held the key to his happiness.

"What are you doing?" She grinned.

"Tomorrow you'll humor me by letting me buy you an ob-

scenely big ring, but for tonight, let's settle this once and for all."
He squeezed her hand. "Will you marry me, Mallory?"

"This can't be about you feeling possessive or wanting to prove a point to me."

"It isn't. Entirely." He grinned back. "I'll admit there's a part of me that wants to make you mine so no other man can have you. But there's only one reason I'm asking."

"Which is?"

"I want to spend the rest of my life with you. You make me feel real. You ground me. I try to imagine life without you, and I can't."

She knelt down in front of him and ran her hands through his short hair. "I can't believe you're mine. All mine."

"I am. Wholly. Completely. In your hands."

She understood what it had taken for him to say those words, for him to trust her, open to her, let her love him. "And I'm in yours," she whispered. "Happily. Forever after." She kissed him. "Of course I'll marry you, *querido.*"

SEVERAL WEEKS LATER, lying in bed wrapped in each other's arms, Roberto and Mallory shared a quiet laugh at the newspaper clipping Patricia had sent them. The picture showed Mallory and Roberto holding hands next to the No. 507 car, she dressed in a Molloy Cycle T-shirt and cap and he in his red-and-white uniform. The headline read, *Engaged: America's Sweetheart Tames Racing's Biggest Playboy!* But the subhead read, *Or Has Mallory Dalton Been Fooling Us All Along?*

"They finally got it right." Roberto leaned over and kissed Mallory.

"On both counts," she murmured against his lips.

* * * * *

*For more thrill-a-minute romances set against
the exciting backdrop of the NASCAR world, don't miss*

*OVER THE WALL by Dorien Kelly
Available in May.*

For a sneak peek, just turn the page!

STACY EVANS CHECKED her makeup for the third time since pulling into the parking lot at Cargill-Grosso Racing. Cosmetics were low on her list of worries, but at least they were something she could control. The butterflies on caffeine flitting around in her stomach clearly had minds of their own. There would be no taming them until she exited this job interview.

Stacy wanted the team's newly posted position as Kent Grosso's crew strength and conditioning coach so very much. Too much, really. While she loved NASCAR and the excitement that swirled around it, that wasn't the big reason she was here. The personal stuff, though, she had to push aside if she had any hope at all of remaining collected through her talk with team manager Nathan Cargill. With her lack of an exercise physiology degree—heck, any kind of college degree for that matter—she was lucky to have been asked to interview.

Sure that her mascara hadn't produced a single stray fleck, that her lip gloss was perfectly applied and that she wasn't about to commit one of those interview atrocities of giving a direct and sincere speech about her qualifications with a bit of her morning granola stuck between her teeth, she turned her rearview mirror back into position. Before exiting the car, Stacy spoke her employment mantra.

"Overdeliver," she said in a firm voice.

So far, that mantra had given her the confidence and drive to escape the dark chaos that had been life growing up with Brenda, her mother, and to move up from being an assistant at a crowded Charlotte gym to having her own packed list of wealthy, private clients who swore that Stacy was a miracle worker of a fitness trainer.

Overdeliver. What else could a girl do? Except maybe fail, and no way on earth would she do that. She'd watched her mother fail, and it had been an ugly lesson that she had no intention of repeating.

Before stepping under the shady portico, Stacy paused for three deep, cleansing breaths. Maybe it was a little odd that a high-energy, overdeliver-type girl thrived on yoga, but she figured there were worse personality quirks out there.

The building's reception area was empty of people, except for a receptionist. She smiled up at Stacy from her seat behind a mahogany desk.

"Good morning," she said.

Stacy was afraid that her answering smile was nervous around the edges. "Hi, I'm Stacy Evans. I have a nine-o'clock appointment with Nathan Cargill."

The receptionist checked the computer monitor in front of her, then said, "Welcome, Ms. Evans. You'll find Mr. Cargill and Mr. Noble down that hallway, in the first conference room on your left."

Stacy felt her butterflies kick into high gear. While it made good sense that Kent Grosso's crew chief, Perry Noble, would be involved in the decision, no one had mentioned that he'd be in the interview. Both Cargill and Noble in the same room smacked of a "bad cop/worse cop" kind of interview.

"Thank you," Stacy said to the receptionist.

As she followed the route the other woman had directed, Stacy pulled back her shoulders, pinned on a smile and prepared to do battle. Heaven knew she'd survived worse.

The door to the conference room was slightly ajar…just enough that she could see Nathan Cargill seated at the far end of the long conference table. As she took in his features, her butterflies suddenly lurched to a halt and began a new dance. This one shimmied with the rhythm of attraction. Stupid butterflies.

Stacy had never thought about whether she had a "type" of man that attracted her. Now, with no thought at all, she knew.

Nathan Cargill was totally, absolutely and undeniably her type.

REQUEST YOUR FREE BOOKS!

2 FREE NOVELS PLUS 2 FREE GIFTS!

SPECIAL EDITION®

Life, Love and Family!

YES! Please send me 2 FREE Silhouette Special Edition® novels and my 2 FREE gifts (gifts are worth about $10). After receiving them, if I don't wish to receive any more books, I can return the shipping statement marked "cancel." If I don't cancel, I will receive 6 brand-new novels every month and be billed just $4.24 per book in the U.S. or $4.99 per book in Canada. That's a savings of at least 15% off the cover price! It's quite a bargain! Shipping and handling is just 25¢ per book*. I understand that accepting the 2 free books and gifts places me under no obligation to buy anything. I can always return a shipment and cancel at any time. Even if I never buy another book from Silhouette, the two free books and gifts are mine to keep forever.

235 SDN EEYU 335 SDN EEY6

Name	(PLEASE PRINT)	
Address		Apt. #
City	State/Prov.	Zip/Postal Code

Signature (if under 18, a parent or guardian must sign)

Mail to the **Silhouette Reader Service:**
IN U.S.A.: P.O. Box 1867, Buffalo, NY 14240-1867
IN CANADA: P.O. Box 609, Fort Erie, Ontario L2A 5X3

Not valid to current subscribers of Silhouette Special Edition books.

Want to try two free books from another line?
Call 1-800-873-8635 or visit www.morefreebooks.com.

* Terms and prices subject to change without notice. Prices do not include applicable taxes. Sales tax applicable in N.Y. Canadian residents will be charged applicable provincial taxes and GST. Offer not valid in Quebec. This offer is limited to one order per household. All orders subject to approval. Credit or debit balances in a customer's account(s) may be offset by any other outstanding balance owed by or to the customer. Please allow 4 to 6 weeks for delivery. Offer available while quantities last.

Your Privacy: Silhouette is committed to protecting your privacy. Our Privacy Policy is available online at www.eHarlequin.com or upon request from the Reader Service. From time to time we make our lists of customers available to reputable third parties who may have a product or service of interest to you. If you would prefer we not share your name and address, please check here. ☐

SSE09

Love Inspired

Firefighter Nic Carano relishes his bachelor lifestyle. Then he loses his heart to a rescued baby. And when he meets the infant's lovely aunt, Nic starts considering love, marriage…and a baby carriage. But after all Cassidy Willis has been through, she's not convinced she wants to spend her life with someone whose life is always in danger.

Look for

The Baby Bond
by
Linda Goodnight

Available May wherever books are sold.

Steeple Hill®

HISTORICAL

INSPIRATIONAL HISTORICAL ROMANCE

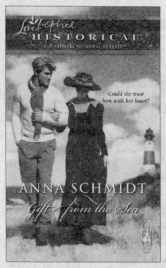

Through the dark days of the Great War a steadfast faith kept nurse Maggie Hunter going. But her fiancé's death shattered her trust in God. Now an injured man has washed up on the shores of Nantucket, and to save him Maggie must put more than her skill and dedication on the line. Stefan Witte is determined to make Maggie believe and forgive again...even if it means his life.

Look for

Gift from the Sea

by

ANNA SCHMIDT

Steeple Hill®

Available May wherever books are sold.

www.SteepleHill.com

LIH82811

Ingrid Weaver

WITHIN STRIKING DISTANCE

Becky Peters longs to find her birth family, and when a prominent NASCAR family reveals that their daughter was kidnapped at birth, Becky dares to hope. As a result, she hires private investigator Jake McMasters to kick the search into high gear. But someone with a deadly secret is watching their every move…and will stop at nothing to keep the truth buried.

Available August 2009 wherever books are sold.